THE SNOW COW

— Read this and you'll never sleep again!

Martin Kochanski *Mark.*

UNIVERSALIS PUBLISHING

First published in 2009 by
Universalis Publishing Ltd
81 Cambridge Mansions
London SW11 4RX

2 4 6 8 10 9 7 5 3 1

A CIP catalogue record for this book
is available from the British Library.

ISBN 978-0-9563199-0-6

Cover design by Emily Fox.

Printed in Great Britain by the MPG Books Group,
Bodmin and King's Lynn

THE SNOW COW

Martin Kochanski has skied, clambered and walked all over the French and Swiss Alps, the Tirol and the Dolomites. He can climb 100 metres in 10 minutes but comes down rather faster. His dark and controversial play *Morgan's Boys* received critical acclaim at the Edinburgh Fringe in 1998. *The Snow Cow* is his first published fiction.

CONTENTS

The Snow Cow

Alpine villages are there because of alpine pastures. Ever since people have lived in the mountains, the herds have been driven up to the fresh new grass as the snow melts, and brought back down to the cowsheds in the valleys before the storms begin in the autumn.

Times change, and most places don't do it any more. Alpine pastures are a problem rather than a resource: Zermatt actually has to hire goats to keep the grass down. Poor places like Arosa can't afford to hire anything, and there the ancient customs carry on. The cows go up in the spring and the cowherds go with them. In the daytime they milk their cows and make cheese out of the milk. They organize cow-fights, and they weave chaplets of mountain flowers for the victors to wear on their horns. At night they play at keeping watch for wolves and bears, and dream of going out to conquer the world.

Throughout the summer, therefore, the walker will find cows readily available whenever he needs one to add picturesqueness to his photographs of the view. The nervous walker will attract whole groups of them, gathering round and staring with their deep liquid eyes, politely dribbling green slime from the corners of their mouths and scenting the air with their warm sweet breath.

On the twenty-first of September everything changes. On that day summer ends and autumn begins. On that one day, every cow must leave the mountain. The senior cows are wreathed with flowers and the stampede begins. The rocks echo with frightened bellowings and the thunder of hooves. Walkers hide in the mountain huts, and when they come out again all is quiet. The only signs that there were ever cows at all are hoofprints and cow-pats and a few crushed flowers.

One year the autumn storms came early, and on the day of the equinox the air was full of water. Great sprays of rain flew downwards, sideways, even upwards in the turbulence, and a thick mist covered everything. But the immemorial custom must not be changed. The paths became streams of mud in which the terrified beasts slipped, bumped, tripped, fell and picked themselves up to struggle onwards. The men could not use their radios in the high winds – there was no way to hear what was being said – so it was a relief to find, when they had got down, that they were all safe and only one cow was missing.

There was no going back to look for her, not for one cow, not in that storm, not that day, or the next, or the next. By the time the storm was over, there was no point in going back: it was too late. They would find nothing but black birds circling a heap of carrion – a few days later, nothing but a cloud of flies. The cow's owner was a popular man and everybody chipped in to help him with the loss. Then they all settled down to mend dripping roofs, watch TV, and wait for the tourists to come and pay for everything.

But the cow was not dead. She had not even broken a leg. She had simply been frightened and badly winded, and by the time she had finished feeling sorry for herself and looked around her, she was alone and lost in the mist. Everyone else had gone. She found shelter under an overhanging rock and lay down to await developments. She was a practical cow.

When there is not enough grass left to feed a hundred cows, there is still plenty for one. In the still-warm sunshine of early autumn she wandered the meadows and picked delicately at the greenest grass and the most fragrant herbs, with no-one to bully her or steal the nicest plants from under her nose.

Wolves have long been extinct in the Alps, and although bears have recently been reintroduced into the Italian Alps and a couple of inquisitive adolescent males once crossed the border into Switzerland to have a look, they soon went home again. The cow was perfectly safe. As the days grew shorter and the nights grew colder, she found her way to the sheltered caves beside the scree. She slept in them at night while in the ground beneath her feet the marmots hibernated, waiting for spring. She was definitely a practical cow.

The nights grew steadily colder and so did the days. Cold drizzle started to soak the village: on the mountain it fell as snow. It was a good foundation for what promised to be an excellent skiing season, but now the cow had to scrape away the snow to get anything to eat. Her hooves bled, and her horns cracked in the cold. She grew thinner and hungrier. Unlike marmots and unlike bears, cows don't hibernate.

9

Ueli Perren had spots. Ueli Perren was going to be something important one day – he just didn't know what, yet. While he waited to discover what it would be, he was growing a beard to hide the spots and he did whatever odd jobs were around. In Arosa in December, that means hauling a season's worth of supplies up to the mountain restaurants. Ueli's job was at the top, putting things away as they arrived off the chairlift – pallets of pasta, powdered soup, frankfurters, the lot. It was good mindless work that gave him plenty of time to get on with his daydreaming, but all the same he was glad when the time came to knock off for the day and take the last chair down. Once or twice, at the end of the day, he shunted the final pallet to one side instead of unloading it, so as to get home sooner. It was against the rules, but after all he could always put the things away in the morning. Nothing would rot in the freezing cold, and there were hardly likely to be thieves up on the mountain on a winter's night.

And indeed, in the morning, there was last night's pallet ready for him to break open and put away. Nothing was missing, and there were no marks of teeth or beaks or claws to suggest that some wild animal had come in the night and helped itself. It was a pity that Ueli did not notice anything when he lifted a carton of chocolate bars that was much lighter than it should have been. In fact half the packets were empty, because the chocolate had been melted out of them. That was strange in itself, and it was stranger still because there was no melted chocolate on the ground. If Ueli had noticed all this at the time then perhaps things would have turned out differently.

Everyone who skis faces the same big risk. It is not avalanches or rocks or falling off a cliff, it is other skiers. One dark afternoon at the end of January, a skier was hurrying down to catch the last lift home. He fell while going along a narrow path through the trees, but injured only his dignity. The woman who was coming up close – too close – behind him was not so lucky. She collided with him, soared into the air and smashed into a tree. Fortunately the man was a serious person who liked to carry everything with him just in case. He unwrapped one of those space-age survival sheets that look like aluminium foil and reflect the body's heat, and carefully covered his victim to keep her warm. He opened a packet of glucose tablets and gave her one to prevent shock. And he skied down to reach the lift and get help.

When the rescuers came, there was no-one to be seen. The silver sheet was there, and so were the victim's skis, propped up in the snow as a marker; but of the victim herself there was no sign. Disturbed snow showed where she must have dragged herself away, but no-one could see why, nor where she had ended up. They searched among the trees and the boulders but there was no sign of her. Some of the cracks between the boulders were huge, big enough to fall into: that must have been what had happened. A further search the next day found nothing. They made a note to look more thoroughly when the snow melted in the spring.

The season went uneventfully on, as most skiing seasons do. Some of the lift operators reported hearing strange animal noises, but an idiotic rumour of bears was quickly squashed when the Italians reported that all their teenagers were accounted for and safely asleep for the winter. Down in the village, human Italian teenagers, who never sleep, caused the same trouble they did every year. A rich woman from Hamburg lost her dog and made an excessive amount of fuss over it. It had run off barking while she was having lunch up on the mountain and had never been seen again. She was the widow of a diamond merchant and people suspected that she was more upset about the dog's diamond-encrusted collar than about the dog itself. The men who scavenge the mountain in the spring heard that story: they put secret marks on their maps and looked thoughtful.

Least exciting of all, one of old Frau Meier's lodgers left without paying her. This happened from time to time and nobody was surprised, because her house was damp and shaken by passing trains and no-one ever stayed there long. Frau Meier was not even particularly irritated. Her guest had left his passport and credit cards behind, which was mildly curious, she supposed; but she sent them along with the other stuff to her cousin in Zurich. He would know how to turn them into money. Meanwhile, the guest had not been there many days, so his towel was unused and would not need washing. On reflection, though, she thought she had better change the sheets.

In early March something more serious happened. The machinery of an important chairlift went wrong so that the only way of starting it was from the top. Unless the lift operator got up two hours early and climbed the mountain by himself in the dark, someone would have to take the last chair up to the top the evening before, and spend the night in a sleeping-bag. Ueli Perren volunteered, because he had a new laptop and needed a chance to chat on it all night without his parents interfering. Actually his friend Ernst had got the job before him, but after the first night Ernst had complained about being kept awake all night by roaring bears. It was obvious that he had been listening to too much lift men's gossip and smoking too much dope: bears don't roar, they growl. Ueli, who didn't smoke, but surfed, was altogether a safer choice.

Night had fallen, and the lights of the restaurant shone out onto the snow. Ueli finished the big plate of rösti they had left for him, opened his laptop and headed for the chatrooms. He planned to go to sleep eventually, but not for a while yet.

An hour or so later he turned on his laptop's camera in preparation for a video chat. The little blue light next to the camera lit up and Ueli saw his own face staring back at him from the screen. Your face is so familiar to you when it's reversed left-to-right in a mirror, it can be a surprise when you see it the way other people see it. This time it was a pleasant surprise: the beard looked much better than he'd expected. And then, on the screen, in the shadows behind Ueli's face, something moved.

Ueli turned round at once, and from the doorway there was a bump as if something big and heavy had moved back in a hurry. There was silence. Ueli turned back to the screen and sat very still. Slowly the thing he had seen came back. It came closer, until Ueli could see that it was a cow.

13

Ueli turned round very slowly to look at her, and although the cow tossed her head anxiously she didn't try to turn and run. She was very shaggy and she was painfully thin. One of her ears looked as if the frost had got at it. He made a move to stand up, but the cow wheeled in panic, sending chairs flying; so he sat and waited for her to calm down, and thought hard.

She must be starving. The only edible thing within reach was a big packet of paprika-flavoured crisps. It would have to do. Ueli tore it open carefully and threw it over his shoulder onto the floor. On the screen he watched her take a tentative step forward, and then another, and bend her head. There was a rustle and the sound of munching. It didn't last long. The cow looked up; Ueli turned round and she retreated again, but more slowly than before, with the crisp packet still stuck to the corner of her mouth.

She really was hungry, thought Ueli. He felt sorry for her. A single packet of crisps seemed so small and the cow was so large. The restaurant wasn't going to contain much of whatever it was that cows ate – but then he spotted a stack of chocolate bars and he remembered how fond horses are of sugar lumps. Perhaps cows were the same? He took a handful of the chocolates, and unwrapped one or two before he got bored and threw them all on the floor, wrapped and unwrapped together. Cows had teeth, didn't they?

It was funny how things had worked out. He knew now where Ernst's scary noises had come from. Poor Ernst: cows don't roar, they moo. If Ueli had anything to do with it, Ernst's friends would call him 'Moo' for months.

14

Ueli went back to his computer and was soon chatting. Rustling noises behind him showed that the cow was working her way through the wrappers somehow.

'Who's that behind you?' his chat friend asked. And indeed, the rustling had stopped and the cow was standing next to him and looking at the screen. Her bristly whiskers tickled his ear. Her breath smelt like a chocolate milk-shake.

'It's my new girlfriend,' Ueli replied. And then, 'She's licking my ear.'

She was. A dog's tongue is floppy; a cat's tongue is scratchy; but cows' tongues are both slobbery and muscular at the same time. They can use them to pull up a whole bunch of grass at once if they want. The cow licked Ueli's ear and made a deep noise that wasn't quite a moo, more a contented rumbling sound.

It was all pretty disgusting, actually.

It was kind of nice.

The cow's lips started to pull at his hair as if it were grass. That hurt. Ueli slapped her nose to make her stop.

The morning came and the lift didn't start. Ernst's mother saw this through the window and went up to tell her son. Dopey he might be, but he had still done better than that stuck-up clever boy Ueli. But Ernst wouldn't listen. He would only wrap his arms round his head and rock back and forth in misery. 'The bears have got him,' was all he said. 'The bears have got him, the bears have got him.'

A sign went up on the lift saying CLOSED FOR TECHNICAL REASONS and a climber was sent up the mountain to see what had happened.

But when the climber got to the top and started the lift, it stayed closed to the public. Only official people were allowed onto it – the rescue team; a doctor; the police. They found what the climber had found: the door was swinging open, the lights were on and confectionery wrappers were blowing about inside. Outside, a trail of churned-up snow led them some distance away, to where Ueli was. Or most of him.

They took photographs from every conceivable angle and they wrapped up what was left of Ueli and took him down to the station and on to the federal pathologist's office in Chur. They sent an avalanche tracker dog up to see if it could find a trail to follow, but it found nothing. Thinking of dogs reminded them that Mrs Kellerman's missing diamond-encrusted chow had disappeared at the same spot a few days before. A nasty, aggressive beast. They confiscated her documents just in case, and told her not to leave Arosa without permission.

Everybody gathered round the fax machine in the police station and waited to hear what had killed Ueli and half eaten him. No fax came. Instead a courier arrived by the evening train, a grim-faced courier who gave the responsible persons a report to read and stood over them while they read it. Then he shredded and burned the report and left for Chur without saying a word. This was their problem, not his.

The autopsy report was written in clear language that anyone could understand. Ueli had been killed by an animal. The toothmarks on his bones had been analysed. They were not from the teeth of a chow or an Alsatian, nor even from a wolf or a bear. These teeth were blunt, and built for crushing. The teeth of a herbivore.

Switzerland is a country prepared and equipped for every emergency up to and including nuclear war. If invaders had seized Chur and marched up the line to Arosa, there were manuals that said exactly which roads should be blocked and which rock-faces should be blown up to block them. The holes were drilled, the explosives were already in place. But what had just happened was not in any manual.

Some things were simple to decide: the lifts were restarted and Mrs Kellerman was told she was free to go home to Hamburg. For the rest, discussions started and stopped, went on and on and led nowhere. It was complicated. As people talked, the days got longer. Up on the mountain the snow was melting in the most sheltered of the south-facing hollows, and the first new leaves started to sprout. There was not enough grazing for a hundred cows, but there was plenty for one.

The farmers clubbed together to give the Perren family a holiday in Majorca for the week that the cows were due to go up to the mountain pastures. It seemed only kind. The cows went up, puffy and unfit from their winter in the sheds. A hundred cows lumbered up the mountain.

Summer passed, and at the autumn equinox, on a quiet sunny day this time, a hundred and one cows came down.

The extra cow's owner kept quiet. It seemed a bad idea to rake up the old story. He was glad to have her back. She was a productive cow.

The next winter, the joke shop by the station started selling novelty cowbells for people to tie to their ski poles. It was a joke in very bad taste, but no-one complained. What's the point in drawing attention to a tragic event that has never officially happened?

Years have passed and things have moved on. What was once bad taste is now high fashion. Everyone knows the cowbells of Arosa, and this year the most expensive shops are selling a must-have item: a his-and-hers matched pair of cowbells, each pair tuned to an identical note, so that you can find your beloved in the middle of a crowd just by her sound. Unless you're tone-deaf, when it becomes a lot more interesting.

One of the bars is going one step further. It's organizing a singles night for Valentine's Day. They give you a cowbell each, and at the end of the evening there is a mass toboggan ride down the mountain in the dark. When you get to the bottom you tinkle your bell and wait for the exactly matching sound.

Ring your cowbell, listen for the answer, hold out your arms and hope for a warm embrace. But as you wait to feel your new beloved's sweet breath on your ear, remember:

Cows have calves.

Predator

The view from the restaurant at Furgg is a raging chaos of rock and ice. Boulders as big as houses lie tumbled in heaps. The swirling glacier grinds rock against rock, limestone against granite, smashing boulders into stones into pebbles into an abrasive grit that the ice takes back into itself and uses to carve fresh boulders out of the crumbling mountains.

The roar of destruction is deafening, but hurried human beings live in seconds rather than centuries. They hear and see nothing but glacial stillness under a deep blue sky.

Tiny, brightly-coloured figures of skiers dart in and out of the wreckage, oblivious to the violence all around. In winter the place is full of them, but in the summer the mountains are lonely.

The boy sitting by the window thought it all looked like one of those whipped coffee-and-vanilla cream puddings with the brown and white spirals frozen in. Most things looked like food to him: especially, just now, the volcano of spaghetti with tomato sauce that stood on the table in front of him, rising majestically to a grated-cheese-covered peak exactly level with his nose. He was pleased with being first and pleased with grabbing the table with the best view of the glacier, but his friends were late and he was hungry.

Me @Furgg Silas were r u spag gets cold

He pressed Send and commenced a trial excavation on the east face of the volcano.

From across the room a pair of ice-blue eyes watched the boy with something approaching interest. They saw a crazed mass of brown curly hair flattened by a woolly hat and greasy with suntan lotion, and a face that still had its childish softness although it was a lot further away from the feet than it had been a year or so ago. A permanent furrow between the eyebrows suggested puzzlement at the change. The watching eyes considered all these facts but discarded them. They were not relevant. What mattered was much simpler. He was alone, and he was alive.

Half the volcano had disappeared and the remainder was slumping into ruin when the phone beeped:

oi m8 met daf so eat @ suneg ok s

It would help, sometimes, if Silas understood the difference between a text and a crossword puzzle. Still, as messages from him went, this one was pretty clear: the group had met Daphne, and consequently the plan was changed and lunch would be at the Sunnegga restaurant. A bit late to be telling him now. Almost at once the phone beeped again:

4got 2send soz lol enjoy spag cya s

Typical Silas. Honour demanded an immediate reply, to put him in his place:

oic far q2 moron T P O

It wasn't strictly true. He wasn't Totally Pissed Off. In fact he wasn't pissed off at all. If anything, he was relieved that he hadn't bumped into Daphne himself. Daphne was round and sweet and huggable and she smelt nice when you sat next to her at meals, but on skis she was a menace on anything steeper than a pool table. Silas was welcome to her and to the geriatric slopes of Sunnegga. Even the food there was inferior.

By now the volcano was utterly extinct and the epic glass of Coke was empty. It was time to stagger out into the sunshine – the weather was too good to waste time indoors. Most people had already gone: even the grizzled tobacco-smelling marmots at the next table had hoisted their heavy backpacks and their radios and stumped off to take it out on some innocent bit of virgin snow. Near the back of the room a girl in an orange ski suit was gazing contemplatively towards him and the window. Her eyes followed his movements as he closed his boots, unfolded himself upright and self-consciously crossed the slippery tiled floor to the stairs – without slipping, flailing wildly, or pulling neighbouring tables down on top of him. "A world first," Silas would have said. Which would have been unfair.

A short traverse brought the boy to a button lift up to one of those pistes that they make brochures out of. It was in shade, but only just. Every turn you made, you kicked up a plume that caught the sun and made a blinding white arc, dazzling against the dark blue sky. The air was so cold that if you looked carefully you could see it glittering with floating crystals of ice.

Directly down the line of the hill, almost in the path of the button lift, a Really Serious Boarder was playing a one-man game of frisbee, throwing it up in the air and shooting down the hill to overtake it, catch it and throw it again. To one side, in a sunny corner, some less serious boarders were imitating mushrooms, heads down, feet up, using their snowboards as sunshades, waiting for the moment when some mysterious flocking instinct would seize them all at once and send them off on some new migration.

The piste had been gratifyingly steep at the start, but now it was flattening out as it drew breath to flow past the bottom of the button and pour on, down, over the edge and out of sight.

The boy tried not to look.

It wasn't the kind of vertigo that other people had. He had no trouble with *high* places. He could stand at the top platform of the cable car and calmly look through the perforated metal floor onto the trees a hundred feet below. He could ski the almost vertical bits beneath the lift stations, and enjoy it. He could do almost anything, as long as he could see the bottom. But put him on a hill of just the wrong shape – a gentle grass-covered hill that anybody could climb – a hill that curved smoothly innocently out of sight until the next thing you saw was a distant view... put him on that hill and if he didn't shut his eyes quickly his soul would roll away from him, faster and faster down the smooth slope until it bounced out of sight into the invisible abyss. He could resist for a short time, but sixty seconds' exposure to exactly the wrong kind of curve would see him on all fours, hugging the ground and clutching the grass to save himself from falling out into the void.

There'd been that time on Gornergrat a couple of days ago, when a perfectly innocuous bit of blue run, butter wouldn't melt in its mouth, children of six were doing it at top speed backwards, had ended in a fringe of trees at the bottom, and, just beyond them, the village in the valley, three miles distant. He'd stared at the tips of his skis until he'd gone cross-eyed with the effort of not looking at the view, but it hadn't helped. In the end he'd had to take them off and slide humiliatingly down on his bottom. He knew it must have been truly terrible because Silas (coming up behind) had seen the whole thing and had never mentioned it to anyone or made the smallest joke about it: Silas, who could make a badly wiped nose last a day and a half.

The piste map said there was a red run somewhere beyond the edge. The piste map was right, he knew. It was a really nice red run too. Wide, with some decently steep patches here and there as it wound down through the woods. He knew because he'd been there with the crowd – but that had been on a misty day with no view. Today there was no mist and there was a view. The edge was clearly visible, and then the same village he'd seen last time, only now it was five miles away, not three, and more than a mile beneath him.

Already his legs were getting self-conscious. Already he was beginning to ski like Daphne, using the whole width of the piste and running out of speed when he got to the edge, so that proper turning was impossible. He had already started to sideslip downwards to try to avoid having to turn at all. And he wasn't even near the bottom yet.

From not very far away the girl's ice-blue eyes watched his fear. The fear made no sense. The eyes did not understand it but still they went on watching, with hungry compassion.

Seeking something for his gaze to hold onto to avoid sliding into the infinite, the boy caught sight of some rocks a little way below and to the right. There was something orange standing next to them. It was the girl he had seen in the restaurant. Grateful to have something to look at other than the village, he kept his eyes on her. A narrow path seemed to lead past the rocks, a nice finite path with no soul-draining view beyond it. As he came close, the girl moved off down the path, slowly. He took it to be an invitation. He turned pale and hot in quick succession. She had been waiting for him.

He followed her. The path was too narrow to need anything clever in the way of technique. When it went downhill he went faster, then it went uphill a little and he slowed down. The fact someone was in front of him meant that it wasn't all about to end catastrophically. On his left, the ragged rock wall protected him from panic while letting him see that they were skiing round the edge of a vast glacier-filled bowl. He had never seen anything so huge. It was an arena for a rock concert bigger than the world had ever seen. He could imagine the sound check echoing and resounding from rock-face to rock-face. All he could really hear in the deep silence was the faint crumping sound of the soft snow under his skis, but the sense of echo was so strong he could imagine the band already tuning up, on instruments too deep for any human being to hear.

The orange ski suit stayed a hundred yards ahead, sometimes a little further, sometimes a little closer. It would probably have been hard to keep his eyes off that tight orange bottom flowing so smoothly through the landscape but he didn't know because he didn't even try.

The path seemed well-travelled. From time to time a couple of ski tracks would dodge away to the left and vanish behind the rocks – obviously left by snow–raping nutters like the ones he'd sat next to at lunchtime.

The girl was suddenly closer. She had paused at a point where the rocky margin petered out and a virgin snowfield lay at an angle before them, like a quilt sliding off a bed. He wanted to shout to her that he didn't know how to ski powder, but before he got close enough she was off into it, floating down in a curve through the tilted snow. His eyes followed her, and his body followed his eyes.

There is something about being a man skiing behind a woman, even when you are very young and don't have much idea of what you'd do if you caught up with her. Following a man, it is permissible to show weakness. You can admit you can't do things. If that reveals him to be stronger than you, well, it is the duty of the strong to look after the weak. If the worst comes to the worst, you can sit down and use your phone to ring for the helicopter rescue. But ski behind a woman, and there is no escape. Your genes take over. What she does, you do; and if it ends up killing you – so what?

There is nothing sexual about it, she can even be your mother or your sister: if the woman leads, you have to follow. It's built in. The boy followed because he could do nothing else.

The worst thing you can do when skiing powder is to put your weight too far forward, bury your tips and go flying head over heels. The other worst thing is to put your weight too far back so that your skis run away with you. The *other* other worst thing is to attempt to turn using the techniques you learned on the pistes. You can end up scattered across quite a lot of mountainside, doing that.

Thus, as it turned out, having your body completely rigid with terror was really quite a good strategy. All the muscles locked themselves in panic until the body might as well have been a plank of wood, solid and moving as a single mass. And then, as you desperately watched the orange ski suit curving round, passing through the vertical and starting to come back across the slope on the opposite tack, you naturally turned your head to follow her. And turning your head turned your shoulders, and turning your shoulders shifted your weight – just a little, just enough for your skis to do the same thing she was doing.

A good hundred feet lower down and facing in the direction they'd originally started from, the girl found another path with shallower snow on it, and stopped. The boy came up behind her, thinking 'I'll never do that again' and 'Let's do it again now' in exactly equal proportions. This time the girl in the orange ski suit did not move off as he got closer. Even when he misjudged his speed a little and had to ski to a stop above her and step down, she waited, leaning on her poles and looking out at the view.

His back was wet with sweat and his muscles ached as if he'd been rowing all day. He took out a piece of chocolate, broke it in two, put one piece in his mouth and offered the other piece to the girl. She declined it with a smile: a delicate happy smile with tiny pearly white teeth and a small pink tongue somewhere behind them; and above the smile, only the single curve of her wrap-round goggles reflecting the mountains stark against a golden-black sky.

She pulled off her headband and her dark hair streamed down onto her shoulders. With both poles she pushed off hard, along this new path that was surely leading back to the red run. He followed close behind, imitating her every move so that in the end it was hard to tell whose body was whose, and whose mind was moving whose legs. He looked about him, up, round, across, even down into the steep drop at his side. Skiing with her, he could not understand how he could ever have been frightened of any of this.

Thus it was that when the next corner arrived and the path suddenly came to an end, his soul did not dive down into the depths. It floated, it flew, it soared, it echoed from wall to wall of the immense arena. The girl's work was done. The orange of her suit became just one more colour to add to the glitter of the ice crystals that filled the air. Of the boy, a few irrelevant details described a long curve down to the uncaring rocks below.

In the summer, the mountains would not be lonely any more.

Eve

The toughest time of a chalet holiday is dinner on the first day.

It doesn't matter how tired you are. You have to sit round the table, upright and elegant, just like the picture in the brochure, and you have to make upright and elegant conversation on upright and elegant subjects – just like the brochure. If you don't do it, you don't get fed: it's that simple. The flames of the candles burn holes in your sun-fried eyes but you can't close them to protect them, because in 20 seconds you'd be asleep. You have to keep your eyes open. You have to inspect the other guests and calculate. Who is going to be your lifelong friend for the week? Whom will you spend your time avoiding?

On the other side of the table from Eve, the woman with a face like a disapproving handbag had made her decision already. Her whole body said it, the way she sat slightly twisted, leaning a little to her right; because on her left sat a black man.

Now, these things certainly have their place. They give a pleasing variety to news broadcasts and make us feel good about ourselves. When you find them running the cheaper

28

kinds of market stalls it shows the value of hard work, thrift and enterprise among the lower orders. These things have their place – when they *know* their place. But *this* black man, this black man *here*, this *rich* black man with his expensively understated clothes, well dressed, well spoken, educated, intelligent, athletic, and an unparalleled lover...

Eve wondered if she was ever going to stop being glad that she'd married him.

Even as he was now, imploded with exhaustion and despair, he was the most beautiful thing in the room. From the moment she'd first seen him, she had known this was a prize she had to win. She had planned her campaign and she had executed it well. Later, as a bonus, she had found that the prize had been worth winning, as well. Even after a day like today, it still was.

On the other side of Mrs Face-Like-a-Handbag, now, that must be Mr Handbag.

'No, don't look at him, please, it really doesn't help.'

It was a droopy voice. Hollow now, but once upon a time it must have been beautiful. Eve's neighbour was old but still sleek. Thin skin that revealed the blood beneath. Thin lips and small watery eyes. Thinning hair carefully arranged to cover his skull. With his domed forehead and his skinny neck, he reminded Eve of a friendly tortoise. He smelt a little musty, as if someone had put him away in a drawer without ironing him properly first.

'Don't try to look at him. *He isn't there.* Look at *me*, my dear, and try to tell me one single thing about his appearance.

'No? Not even one? Of course not. The man doesn't have presence, my dear, he has *absence*. A commanding absence. A man like that, when he walks into a room, people start noticing the pattern on the wallpaper.'

Half-way through a spoonful of soup, Eve retained her dignity with an effort; and the soup. He was so exactly right.

Encouraged, her neighbour went on. 'He's told me his name. Carefully. He's told me twice. And I still can't remember it. It's hopeless. One of those suburban names, you know. And his conversation. Any moment now, if I catch his eye, he'll start telling me about his new electric garage-opener.' He took an appreciative spoonful of his sorrel soup and dabbed his mouth precisely with a folded corner of his napkin. 'Our chalet girl can't help me, she's up and down and doing things the whole time, she can't defend me, but you will, won't you? I'm Daniel.'

'How do you do, Daniel? I'm Eve.'

'Ah, Eve, the first woman, the *first* of names. Eve, my dear, the pleasure is entirely mine. And your…?' His eyes flicked discreetly towards the far corner of the table.

'My husband, Ignatius.' It felt good saying it. It was a simple pleasure; and a new one. Also, she was having a race. So far Ignatius had managed to say 'my wife' far more times than she had said 'my husband.' He'd held on to the tickets and passports all through their journey, which had naturally given him more opportunities. Which was cheating, really. It was time to restore the balance a little.

'We were married yesterday.'

Eve thought she had seen all possible reactions to them as a couple. There was envy mixed with desire. There was desire mixed with envy. There was the frank and open appreciation that had made a diner at a jazz club in New York send a bottle of wine to their table 'for being such a beautiful couple.' She'd been wearing her red dress that night. At Bradley's or Brantley's, something like that.

The look that had come into Daniel's eyes was none of these. It was new and she couldn't place it at first. She remembered seeing it somewhere recently – and then it came to her. Not only the same look but the same eyes and even the same table: the not-yet-named Daniel watching them having tea after skiing, neither envious nor desiring, but deeply interested. It was the intense calculating look of a chess grandmaster analysing a position.

'So this is your honeymoon? My dear, I felicitate you both.' The words were uttered on autopilot: his mind was clearly elsewhere. Then the next course arrived, and Daniel turned his attention to the best way of eating roast guinea-fowl.

When their conversation started again, it was altogether more relaxed. They played at constructing biographies of the other guests. Mr and Mrs Handbag lived in Carshalton, they decided. Neither Daniel nor Eve was exactly sure where Carshalton was, but it sounded perfect. The wordless spiky snowboarder on Eve's right was Josh ('all snowboarders are called Josh, my dear, it's one of the rules') and his companion, so overawed by the grown-ups and the elegant surroundings that she never looked up from her plate, must be a monosyllable: Bee or Dee or Fee or something.

And next to her...

'Forgive me, my dear, but does your husband always look this grim when he's just been married?'

'Invariably.' Eve ended the game abruptly by slamming the door in Daniel's face. This was not for strangers. The first rule of marriage is absolute solidarity. Whatever troubles we have, they are ours and the world has no right to see them.

Not that it was trouble, really. And certainly not trouble *between* them. It was just that – she was annoyed with herself for letting something so trivial get to her – it was just that she'd heard so much about Ignatius's prowess on skis. His friends had told her all about it. He would take them on intense two-day raids on Chamonix. He'd take potential clients too, so they could see what he was made of before he asked them to trust him. A man for whom nothing was steep or narrow enough, a man who wouldn't touch snow if there were rocks and ice to be had, a man whom people would trust with their lives even after he'd tried to kill himself and them.

It wasn't at all what she'd married him for, but it was certainly why she'd suggested a skiing honeymoon. She'd looked forward to a blitz of skiing, an orgasm of physicality. She'd pictured herself marooned with him on some pinnacle, burying her face in his sleeve and being guided by him from the impossible to the possible and from the possible to the doable, and safely home from there. Her precise, independent, lawyer's mind revolted at the melodrama, but it still made her feel warm, all through.

And then – and then – so far from bashing the blacks (always said in a voortrekker 'beshing-de-blex' South African accent) or riding the reds (New Zealand accent, now), he wasn't even screwing the blues (deepest Australian). Not unless you counted screwing them *up*. All day he'd skied like a hairdresser with two left boots, until on Unterrothorn – *Unterrothorn*, for God's sake, Unterrothorn where the kids' toboggan playground was – he'd frozen rigid at the very top. Another minute and he'd have got out of his skis and carried them up to the cable car and gone down in it, except that a man near them – she'd never seen who – had muttered 'nookie-free zone tonight' in a carefully audible aside, and with death in his heart Ignatius had leant on his poles and shut his eyes and shoved himself forward.

He hadn't turned, not once, not all the way down. He'd juddered over the tops of the moguls until it seemed his teeth would fall out; but he'd stayed upright somehow and stayed alive through all of it and when Eve (skiing rationally) had eventually got to the station at the top of the Sunnegga underground railway she'd found him standing there, calm, skis in hand, waiting to go down with her in the train. Eve wanted to hug him to pieces and wring his silly neck, both at the same time, but her eyes were too full of tears to do either.

So now here he was in the corner wrapped in smouldering negritude, like a statue carved out of basalt, like a black hole swirling deep inside its own event horizon, content that Mrs Face-Like-a-Handbag was avoiding him and that the boarderkids on the other side spoke no human language. Nobody was to be allowed to see into his world just at the moment, that was certain; but Eve's heart was in there with him already. He was her husband.

Definitely Daniel had gone too far. Eve turned back to him, and in a Chelsea-drinks-party voice of triple-lacquered superficiality asked him what he did.

'*Do*, my dear?' His tone said that he had expected better things of her but was too polite to show it. 'I roam, my dear. Here and there.'

He put down the fork with which he had been trying to crack open a dark chocolate shell without catapulting bits of apricot purée around the table. 'I make things happen for people. I suppose you could call me a kind of magician.'

From his pocket he took a small plastic bag containing a few capsules of the kind that antibiotics come in. One end white, the other green. A cardboard label attached to the packet said FAME PILLS.

'To become famous, take one. Take two to become world-famous.' He smirked. '*Can help relieve the symptoms of unwanted obscurity. It is dangerous to exceed the stated dose.*'

To Eve, this was nonsense. 'Do they work?' she asked, for want of anything sensible to say.

'No,' said Daniel, and took a small mouthful of almond paste.

Eve felt the conversation slipping frustratingly out of her grasp. It felt like trying to pick up a quail's egg with chopsticks. Nothing made any sense, and yet she felt an important message was being passed. If only she could work out what it was.

'A pill for every ill,' said Daniel in a satirical tone, turning his attention to the chocolate shell once more and using his spoon as well as his fork. 'Love, money, courage, strength, potency, skills, power. People turn to me for many things.'

'Even skiing ability?' Flippancy was always a safe tactic.

'Even that,' said Daniel. He sounded perfectly serious. Somehow she was playing into his hands, without even knowing what the game was.

Sparring with Daniel was better than talking garage doors with Mr Handbag, but ultimately it was vacuous, and she was tired. Eve declined coffee, got up from the table, and went upstairs to bed, with Ignatius in tow. Ignatius was giving a good imitation of there being nothing wrong at all. Solidarity went both ways. When he tried, Ignatius could give very good imitations of there being nothing wrong.

Eve knew her Ignatius. When he pushed himself too far and something went wrong, he didn't just crumple, he collapsed in ruin – collapsed in every respect. Then there was nothing to do except wait for the pieces to come back together by themselves. In the end they always did. But 'in the end' was later, and now it was now, and Eve knew what she wanted – needed – from Ignatius now. If he had still been her boyfriend she would have taken it, regardless of his state. She knew how. But as a friend of hers had told her (and she hadn't believed it), marriage changes everything. He would never again be her boyfriend. She and Ignatius were 'we' now – and where is the 'we' in 'I want'?

She couldn't *use* Ignatius. But equally, how could she curl up away from him in perfect self-sufficiency – 'if you can't be my stud, be my hot-water bottle'? He deserved more than that. He was her husband.

How unfair it was that men, not women, had the gift of instinctively knowing how to meet vulnerability with just the right kind of tenderness: 'Nookie-free zone tonight.'

Ignatius came back from the bathroom. Not her man of steel, more like a feather-filled bolster, with a brave smile on its face that Eve could see right through. It made her want to start crying and never stop.

Her lawyer's mind had hit a dead end, so her body took over. It knew what to do.

The most private part of an African is his head. Eve's fingers followed the neatly tied lines in Ignatius's hair, now going bump-bump-bump over the tight knots, now slinking along the furrows between.

Half lying on her side, Eve traced the outside edges of his lips. She rested a knuckle on each of his cheekbones and delicately, delicately, delicately, she smoothed his eyebrows with her thumbs.

The intervals between the strokes grew longer and longer. You could never really say 'here, this is the last one.' It was like those silly phone conversations you have when neither of you says anything for twenty minutes but neither of you can put the phone down and break the connection. It was like a sentence without a full stop.

It was actually bloody uncomfortable.

Ignatius was always doing this. Just as she was drifting off to sleep wrapped and surrounded and supported by him, he'd announce that his arm was going numb and he'd thrash and push and pull and then they'd have to begin sorting themselves out again from the beginning.

Eve gritted her teeth and stayed where she was. Perhaps it wasn't going to be as uncomfortable as all that, this giving of comfort. Perhaps…

Her doze was interrupted by a violent jerk from her legs.

All skiers have legs. They are a menace. You spend the whole of the first day teaching them how to behave on skis, and at night, when you're in bed and relaxed, they take the opportunity to show you how well they've learnt their lesson. So you wake up and you calm them, you doze off – and there they are again, twitching and jumping down yet another imaginary run. Nothing helps, not even getting blind drunk before bed. It just has to be endured.

Now that the delicate moment was shattered, there was no reason not to get properly comfortable. Ignatius evidently thought the same. In a series of clear, clean, this-is-not-erotic-I-am-only-rearranging-us moves, he laid her head on his shoulder and enveloped her hand definitively in his.

Their legs could ski all night if they liked; but now they would be skiing together.

A disturbed night always made Eve bright and efficient in the morning. She came downstairs early and found Daniel at his breakfast. Enfolded in a decadent silk-and-cashmere paisley dressing-gown, he was just cracking the shell of a soft-boiled egg. His hair was more optimised than ever and his nails looked as if he had been polishing them.

'How much?' Eve asked, briskly.

Daniel looked up with an expression of polite enquiry.

'Skiing ability. How much? What are your fees?'

Daniel returned his attention to his egg. He meticulously picked up each fragment of broken shell and piled them all in the bottom left-hand corner of the saucer. With the edge of his spoon he cut through the membrane and removed the first spoonful of egg-white. He began to speak. His maddeningly slow discourse was punctuated with alternate mouthfuls of egg and bites from the thin parallel strips of buttered toast on the plate next to him.

'My dear,' he said, 'I don't like this modern business of selling time in exchange for money. It's really nothing but prostitution. I give you seconds – minutes – hours of my life, my *own* life, my *irreplaceable* life, and you offer me *bits of paper* in exchange? My time, which I'll never get back again?

'Let us be more imaginative, my dear. Give me time for time. If we're exchanging gifts, let's at least exchange gifts of equal value.

'In the old days I suppose I could have demanded your eternal soul, but to be honest, my dear, it might not be worth waiting for. And people live so *long* nowadays.'

Having conjured up a satisfyingly sinister atmosphere, Daniel removed the empty shell from its egg-cup and crushed it a little, just a little: not enough to kill it, but enough to make it unable to roll away.

He started his second egg and began to speak in a more businesslike voice. 'Let us be simple, my dear. I expect it will take me an hour or so to make your husband as strong and potent as he has ever been. Perhaps longer, perhaps shorter, but for the sake of argument let us say an hour.

'So, my dear, an hour for an hour, shall we say? What do you think? An hour of your time for an hour of mine? An hour of your time for a lifetime of married bliss?'

Eve was losing patience. 'Oh, anything you say.'

Daniel's voice grew harsh. 'No, my dear, not *anything*.' His hand gripped her arm loathsomely for an instant. 'An hour for an hour, what do you say?'

'An hour for an hour.' Eve repeated the words.

'Then consider it done,' said Daniel, smiling with pencil-thin lips. 'It will be a pleasure to have been of service to you.' He crushed the second eggshell, slowly, sensuously, until it was utterly flat. 'Consider it done.'

Detaching Ignatius from Eve and attaching him to Daniel proved ridiculously easy to arrange. Eve remembered she had promised to spend the morning skiing with her friend Amanda, who was lithe and blonde and glamorous and having a rocky time in her relationship with an older man. It happened to be a perfectly genuine promise, which she'd nearly forgotten. Amanda really did need Eve's company, so the excuse was not only effective but had the additional merit of being true.

Ignatius accepted the new arrangement without hesitation, so that Eve felt a secret anguish at being trusted so completely. When Daniel suggested keeping Ignatius company that morning, Ignatius demurred on the grounds of incompetence, but Daniel smiled and said 'Are you claiming to be worse than me? How *dare* you try to compete?' and that was that.

Eve was left reflecting that often the reason why women don't understand men's psychology is that it's simpler than anyone can imagine.

Amanda's universe was simple too. It was so simple it was beautiful. In it, everything revolved around Amanda, and Amanda's light, in turn, illuminated everything. Eve found it refreshing to spend time in such an ordered cosmos, even when it turned out that things were not going quite as well as they ought. The older Amanda got, the more important it was to consolidate her future by marrying Louis. Which meant Louis leaving his wife. Which he showed no sign of doing. And although Louis was as generous as ever, there were unexplained absences. If he was spending time with his wife, that was bad; if he wasn't, it was positively sinister.

All this came out bit by bit in the course of a morning of flattering skiing, frequent pit stops, and a lot of looking at boys. Altogether a girls' day out.

About noon there came a text from Ignatius saying they were bashing the blacks at Triftji on the next-door mountain and not to wait for him at lunch, but meet at the restaurant at Ried on the gentle route home from Sunnegga. Evidently Ignatius was able to ski again. The relief was enormous.

Amanda happily agreed to come with Eve. She was as keen to see the magnificent dusky beast Eve had captured as Eve was to show him off.

The restaurant at Ried is where they serve a plum tart that is out of this world. The place was packed tight, but that was irrelevant: blondes always get tables. Being a mistress as well as blonde, Amanda couldn't have the plum tart, but Eve did ('Come on, Amanda, do try a bit, it isn't sweet at all') and they had a schnapps each and they were brilliant and beautiful.

A shadow appeared at the door. Before Eve even looked in that direction her body had already told her who it must be. She raised both arms above her head and Ignatius came to her, seeming to wade breast-deep through the crowd. He put his hands on her shoulders, bent down and kissed her on her lips for no more and no less than half a second. An instant longer, and the result would have been thermonuclear.

Amanda was duly presented and shook Ignatius's right hand. His other hand stayed firmly on Eve. He declined the offer of a drink – no, he was knackered, he needed to get home, it was now or never – and they left. Amanda was left behind. She looked older and tireder than before.

As they went out of the door a hand touched Eve's arm. A creepy touch, somehow; and indeed it was Daniel, looking dwarfish and absurd in a black beanie and mirrored sunglasses. His lips were twisted in what might have been a sort of smile, but he said nothing.

'Triftji five times, woooh!' said Ignatius when they were outside, and he shook his head vigorously like a dog, getting rid of imaginary snow from his hair. Triftji was north-facing and steep and it had moguls that went up to your hip. Testosterone-fuelled twenty-year olds would boast of doing it twice before breakfast. Or three times. Five times was superhero territory. Eve felt that things really were turning out all right after all.

The way home from Ried is a boring boring path. Each time you do it, it's twice as long as it was last time. Ignatius, however, couldn't see why paths had to be boring. He started by skiing directly along it, first with legs wide apart like a beginner, then with knees glued together like an Austrian ski instructor. Then he swung like a pendulum from one extreme edge of the path to the other, and the swing tightened into a short tight muscular thigh-destroying wedel. Then the same but with hips, his idea of how Amanda must ski (and remarkably accurate). The final, tight-buttocked, imitation was of someone Eve hadn't met yet. She wasn't entirely sure she wanted to.

Having exhausted the straightforward possibilities, Ignatius started to make little excursions up the bank to their left, where bored skiers had carved alternative tracks that went up a little way and then back down to the path again. Some of them ended in a little jump. Some of them were steep: and one of those Ignatius started a little too slowly, so that his momentum ran out before he got to the top. He stopped; he started sliding backwards. Eve held her breath anxiously. Faster and faster Ignatius went until he hit the path in reverse gear just where he had left it. Eve breathed out in relief and irritation: he had planned every move from the beginning.

After up, Ignatius tried down. A dive into the woods on the right brought him back up and onto the path with a lovely turn-and-jump and a flat slap of skis onto the path that could be heard a long way off.

A second dive ended abruptly half way, with a muffled thump somewhere out of sight. Eve stopped breathing; but just as she was about to suffocate, a ski came flying up and landed on the path. She caught it before it slid off into the distance, and suddenly everything was all right again. After a while another ski appeared. Eve had to struggle back up the path to get that one. A longer pause. Eventually Eve looked round and saw Ignatius some way down the path, looking innocent and waiting for her to knock the snow off his boots and help him put his skis back on.

There was still quite a bit of the path left to go. Now Ignatius had decided to grow up and be serious. It didn't stop him showing off, though. He skied just behind Eve, holding her in front of him like an ice dancer, one hand on her hip and the other one holding her other arm extended. It was a most unstable position and yet Ignatius was in full control of it, not with his feet alone but with infinitesimal adjustments of his whole body as the snow conditions changed. It wasn't just the power that took possession of her, it was the precision with which Ignatius could apply it.

At last the path was over. They had come to Scotch Corner, so called because of the horrible sticky porridge you had to ski through if you wanted to take the short cut. They separated smoothly and skied it like proper adults, picking their way down the slope together, avoiding the

43

most knee-wrenching bits, and pointing out hazards to each other.

Ignatius stayed normal all the way home. Back in the chalet he refused tea but drank five glasses of water very quickly, and they went upstairs to have their baths.

Ignatius hurled himself face down on the bed and before Eve had got her things together to go to the bathroom he was asleep. It was probably the talent of his she envied the most. When she got back after her bath he was still fast asleep; but as she made her way round the bed a hand caught her thigh, and then another hand caught her head and she was being kissed for a lot longer than the calibrated 0.500 seconds up at Ried, by an Ignatius with wide open sparkling eyes who seemed not to care any more what explosions he might cause. Between them, they somehow avoided ignition, and Ignatius went off to have his bath.

'Marrying you has made me too big for my boots,' Ignatius said as he was drying himself afterwards.

What sort of statement was that?

'Daniel thought it had, and he was right. That was the trouble, you see. The boots. My feet have grown half a size since last year. I couldn't put my weight on them properly. It was agony in the end. He's a clever guy, Daniel.'

'I don't like him,' said Eve.

'Oh, he's old, of course,' said Ignatius, neatly wrapping up a creepy manner, a paisley dressing-gown and meticulously located hair into a single all-purpose explanation. 'But you should see him on those moguls, he skis like he was half his age.'

There was nothing Eve could say, unless she explained everything; which would have been ridiculous.

Whether you thought Ignatius was well-behaved at dinner rather depended on who you were. The chalet girl was delighted, as a music student, to find someone who really loved music and was passionate and knowledgeable about it. Eve realised that his regular visits to Glyndebourne and Covent Garden had been for more than just impressing selected clients. She felt some chagrin at another woman discovering something about her husband that she hadn't known herself, but that was nothing compared to the prospect of spending night after night going to operas with him, going to concerts with him, and letting him teach her a new love.

The effect of the conversation on Mrs Face-Like-a-Handbag was shrivelling. So 'these people' not only used their money to worm their way into luxury chalets in exclusive resorts, 'these people' also went to snobbish places like Glyndebourne. There was an eighteen-year waiting list to become a member at Glyndebourne. She had never been there. She wouldn't. She knew her place. 'These people' should know their place too. They had their own music. They had their hip-hop and their rap. What more did they want?

The big surprise of the evening was Mr Handbag. He lingered shyly on the fringes of the conversation and you could see he longed to be part of it. They were talking about things he had heard of and knew a little about, but he could find nothing to say that seemed interesting enough for the others to want to hear it. In the end he rather weakly asked Ignatius how he came to know so much about music.

That was the only time that night, Eve thought, that she had caught Ignatius deliberately putting a spin on something. He explained that he'd spent a year living with his grandmother when he was 14, and he'd listened to her extensive collection of CDs while making models of World War II warships, 'while I suppose I should really have been out on the streets mugging people.' He said it meekly, without looking at Mrs Handbag at all, so the target was obvious.

Eve happened to know that Ignatius's grandmother's house in Ghana was a place where he couldn't lift a finger without six servants rushing to lift it for him, and where there were no streets of any kind within miles. Uncertainly, Mr Handbag caught Eve's eye. Eve winked. Mr Handbag smiled a crooked smile back at Eve, almost nodding at his wife as he did it. I know she's a monster, he seemed to be saying with resignation, but if I don't love her, who will? A weak man can be a hero too, thought Eve. The idea was new to her. She hadn't seen a marriage like that before.

Ignatius's clowning was all rather fun; but as the evening went on, Eve was more and more oppressed by Daniel's presence. Physically he was remote, at the other end of the table, between the boarderkids, but she knew that he was watching her throughout the meal, calculating. Once, when her gaze accidentally met his, he licked his thin lips.

It had started with drinks before dinner. Somehow – none of her doing – Eve and Daniel had found themselves isolated from the others. She had thanked him politely for being such a help to Ignatius.

'It was a pleasure, I assure you, my dear,' he said; 'and I have another pleasure still to come, I believe? Shall we say, three o'clock tonight? Such a quiet time. I do hate to leave debts outstanding, don't you? You never know, my dear, you may find that you enjoy being with me almost as much as I enjoyed being with your husband. A bientôt!' And he had touched her head, once, lightly.

She could feel that touch still. She had gone away later and brushed her hair, but still she could feel that touch.

So there it was in the end – desire and envy, envy and desire. That had been the solution all along. Desire, fermented into pure poison in the mind of a clever and amoral man; and envy, directing it. He had calculated right. At a time when her body should be approaching liquefaction at the thought of the coming hours with Ignatius, it was hard and tense instead, and her skin was crawling from Daniel's last touch and the possibility of another one.

There was *no* possibility. Look at it rationally. What could Daniel conceivably do? Rattle the door-handle? Pick the lock? Scratch discreetly at the frame? Knock? It was all ridiculous. She would ignore it, whatever it was, and if it couldn't be ignored, she would open the door to him and slam it again so hard they would still be picking fragments of bone out of the wood the next day.

But all this was ridiculous. Nothing would happen. She was married, she was very married, she was faithful without even having to think about it. The trouble was, Daniel knew this as well as she did. Whatever the master chess-player had planned, he had taken all these facts into account already.

There is a kind of wasp that lays its egg in the back of a caterpillar's head. In time a maggot hatches out of the egg and burrows in and eats the caterpillar's brain. Daniel was that wasp.

Eve climbed the narrow staircase to their bedroom, with Ignatius close behind her. She could feel his body humming with tension like a violin string. As each wooden stair creaked under his weight, it sent vibrations up her legs and through her spine. She could feel his eyes on her hips as she climbed each step. And yet, at the same time, she felt the echo of Daniel's lazy, damp glances. She had lost.

A fear deeper than reason undermined the foundations of thought itself. If part of the thrill of Ignatius's touch was that it might have been Daniel's touch but wasn't – if part of the magic of Ignatius's smell was that it might have been damp and musty like Daniel's but wasn't – then Daniel would become part of that night and remain so forever. Even if, by some miracle, thoughts of Daniel did not appear before that moment came when all thought ends, and words like 'Eve' and 'Ignatius' ceased to have separate meanings – if Ignatius proved to be the stronger of the two, as of course he was – still, afterwards, as she came to herself to the sound of the ticking of his watch, each tick would surely bring the same question: 'Is it 3am yet?' 'Is it 3am yet?' Daniel was a wasp, and his egg was hatching.

It was fear that made Eve decide to lie. As she lay in their bed and waited for Ignatius to come to her, she remembered a much younger Eve, inexperienced and in the grip of a passion that neither she nor her lover could control. Sitting with a cold cup of coffee and a crumpled packet of cigarettes, sitting and watching the telephone, prepared to wait all night for it to ring. A young and inexperienced Eve who could not say 'no' – but who, with her last shred of rationality before settling down to her vigil, had unplugged the phone.

So now Eve was strong. She lied. She had no willpower left to say the words 'Not now, we must wait until it's safe.' She had no mind left for the explanations that might have to follow. But words and explanations were unnecessary. As Ignatius approached – she could feel the hairs rise on the backs of her arms as he came closer – she lied smoothly, without the need for words. A gesture, a grimace, a particular way of curling up uncomfortably – they said, 'female issue.' Ignatius understood instantly, as Eve had known he would. Men are squeamish about the way that women's bodies really work, and Ignatius was very much a man. Far too much of a man to think it through or ask questions.

They moved into the positions they had evolved, long before, to deal with this situation. Eve folded in on herself. Ignatius lay close to her, an arm extended above her head and round to the other side, a protective rampart that never actually touched her. She could feel its heat. She wanted to forget everything after all, and let things happen the way they wanted to happen. It would be so easy; but then, afterwards, before even the ticking of Ignatius's watch, what if she heard Daniel's voice? 'Well *done*, my dear!'

Eve felt like screaming. She must have moved, because Ignatius adjusted his position, getting closer while somehow still avoiding the perilous contact. A wall of love round her. She could hear his watch ticking. Each tick was one more step in hope, towards 3am, and battle at last, and victory.

Against all expectation, Eve slept.

Eve awoke, instantly alert. Her mind was clear and clean. It was still dark. An alien blue-green glow from the alarm clock revealed the shapes, no more, of the furniture in the room. She disdained to look to see what time it said. That would be playing Daniel's game.

There was a musty smell as if the bed had been made up with damp sheets. Somewhere a floorboard creaked. The noise came from outside, from the other side of the door. Daniel? Eve remembered how Daniel had touched her arm, and later her head, and she shuddered in loathing at the memory. Inside her, an echo of the shudder came – but there was a little touch of warmth at the end of it.

Women are different from men, an ex-boyfriend of hers had told her (mercifully ex and mercifully brief). Women are different. Drive a wedge between a woman and her body, and you can do what you like with it. And he had demonstrated, actuating her secret levers and buttons, playing whole symphonies on her and in her while all the time talking about football on the phone to a friend.

Daniel's brain-worm had hatched and it was eating its way into her. It was discovering her body's reflexes and working out what they did. Each time she tried to resist, it identified the target she was defending, and so knew more than it did before, about how she worked and what to do to her next. The more Eve struggled, the more Daniel's web tightened around her. The more she resisted, the more complete its victory became.

It seemed that it could never end – and then, without any conscious thought, Eve found she had the answer. 'All right, *my dear*,' she said silently to her attacker. 'You win. Locked doors can't stop you. My resistance only helps you. My strength becomes yours. So now, try my weakness.

'You win. My body is yours. I will stay out of your way. Do what you like. I'm not interested. I won't even be there.

'An hour, we said? I estimate that you have fifty-two minutes remaining. Try not to make too much noise, and let me know when you've finished.'

And Eve put all her courage into the hardest task of her life. To observe her sensations without feeling them, to let whatever happened happen, and not intervene.

Nothing did happen. Time passed, and more time – and still nothing.

Eve realised that all that Daniel had ever wanted was her defeat – her body had merely been his battleground and his weapon. By handing it over to him unconditionally she had abandoned the battle, and where there is no battle there can be no defeat and no victory. Daniel had lost.

Eve felt thirsty, so she got up. The light from the clock was enough to navigate by. She walked quietly towards their bathroom. The wood felt warm under her bare feet.

A floorboard creaked. She reversed her last step and then took it again. A child's trick, when it's learning how it can move about its bedroom at night without its parents hearing. No creak this time, so it must have come from outside. He was there.

To get to the bathroom she had to go past the door of their room. She heard another creak, closer. If I hold my breath, she thought, I'll hear him breathing.

In her mind she flung open the door and beat his silly face into a pulp. His blood and drool covered her fists. He deserved it. He'd started it. It would be ultimate victory.

For him.

As her feet took her past it, Eve saw that the bedroom door had been the final trap. To open it would have been to let Daniel into their night. The more she pounded him, the more he would have become part of this night's story. They would have remembered this night forever, not because of them but because of him; not as their true wedding night but as the night of Daniel. Bloody, broken, disgusting, he would have won.

And what was he? He was nothing.

Eve stepped into the bathroom – and a new story began.

The tiled floor was hard and cold, and it cleared her mind. Her bare feet felt the polished surface, and counted the cracks between the tiles as she walked over them.

A shaft of moonlight came in through a small window high in the wall. Eve ran water into her cupped hands, and drank. She stood upright and looked at herself in the mirror. There was nothing to see. She was a dark shadow against a dark background.

Eve took more water and splashed her face with it. It felt like some sort of pagan ritual: a naked woman, and water flowing in the moonlight. To blunder about hunting for towels would break the magic: Eve wiped her hands on her bare thighs and stepped back into the bedroom.

The smell of mould was forgotten. The air had an interstellar purity. Eve caught a faint distant smell of nutmeg and knew it was the smell of her own body. As she came nearer to the bed the air grew warm, and it carried a new smell, of a healthy animal. A smell that tingled down the back of your neck. It was the smell of Ignatius, her husband.

Eve laid herself precisely down in the centre of the space between Ignatius and the edge of the bed. From somewhere far away in the house there came a metallic sound that might have been the click of a latch.

'Ignatius, my husband,' she thought, 'I was wrong to be strong. When you were weak I should have lived your weakness with you, the way I promised at our wedding. We could have found our way through it together. Instead, I tried to drag you out of it with my own strength, and look where it got me.

'Ignatius, my husband, I was wrong to keep quiet, but I am not afraid. You have vowed to be mine in bad times as well as good, in weakness as well as strength, in foolishness as well as wisdom. I will tell you the whole story tomorrow. If it's still worth telling. If it still matters, then. It will not be my story alone, it will be ours.'

Then Ignatius's arm reached out towards Eve, authoritatively; and nothing mattered any more.

The Long Man

On summer nights the cellar bar at the Post Hotel is the place where climbers and mountain walkers gather to swap stories of the day's adventures and make plans for tomorrow. The wooden floor has been worn into waves by generations of their hob-nailed boots. Its wood-panelled walls are hung with mementos: the photographs of climbers who conquered the peaks and of those who never came back. There is one faded picture in an alcove that always has a tiny glass vase of flowers in front of it. It shows two men and a woman smiling at the dawn at the start of their expedition.

In the winter the bar is a bit of an anomaly. Its stairs are too steep for ski-boots, and once you have changed your clothes after skiing, there are many more vibrant places to go. Dried flowers replace the fresh ones in the vase, and the place smells of dust as much as it smells of polish.

The barman took a bottle out from its hiding-place under the bar, uncorked it, and poured a generous measure into a glass. He added exactly three medium-sized lumps of ice and, just as every night that season, pushed the drink silently across to the tweed-jacketed gentleman who was sitting at the bar. The gentleman in tweed thanked him, just as he had every night that season, and looked across the room to where the only other guest, a young man with red hair, was sitting upright at a table in front of a glass of beer.

'I think he's the one,' he said.

'Are you sure?' said the barman. 'He seems pretty normal to me.'

'What do you want him to look like? Do you want him weeping into his beer or something? That wouldn't be the type I've been looking out for. Not the type at all.'

He held his glass up to the light and watched the pale threads of clear water melting off the ice and making their way down through the straw-coloured whisky. He said quietly to himself, 'If the binding is stronger than the leg, the leg must break.' He shook the glass slightly and the threads swirled, tangled, and broke up, giving the drink a faintly marbled appearance. Slowly, the currents died down and the threads began to establish themselves again. 'If the leg breaks quickly,' he added, 'the joint may be saved.' He contemplated his drink in silence.

'How long have you been coming here?' The barman hadn't meant it to sound that abrupt, but somehow this didn't seem to be the time for politeness.

The man in tweed smiled. It transformed his face, just as an overcast afternoon is transformed when the low sun breaks through the cloud at last. He looked suddenly young – young and looking forward to life – and for a moment his clothes didn't look as if they belonged in a museum. 'As long as that bottle's been there,' he said.

Yes. The bottle. The barman knew about that bottle. At the end of his first week, when he was taking stock, he was sure he'd have to replace it but it still seemed pretty full. Out of interest he'd made a quiet pencil mark on the label. A few days later, when he'd remembered to look, the whisky was still up to his line. He began to watch carefully. At the end of each evening, the level was definitely down, an inch or more if he'd been generous that night. The next morning it was back to normal. He'd tried hiding the bottle so whoever was filling it couldn't find it, but it hadn't made any difference. After that, he'd rather got used to it.

'He still looks normal.' The red-haired drinker was half way through his beer, and absorbed in doing things with his phone. Texts, probably.

'I bet you I'm right,' said the man in tweed.

'How much?'

'That's tricky, isn't it? If I win, you won't see me again to pay me. You won't see either of us again, for that matter. That's a big benefit for you, really, but I don't mind. I'll be happy. And if I lose, you can simply say "I told you so."'

'I told you so.'

'Then, not now.'

'No, I'm simply being polite and saying "I told you so" in advance. If you're here tomorrow night telling me you were wrong and your long wait has to go on, I wouldn't want to rub it in. It wouldn't be fair.'

The cloud was winning its battle with the sun. The man looked no older than before, but he looked tired – very tired.

'I've been wrong before, but this time I *know* I'm right. Anyway, you know, it's something I've got to do.'

'If you say so. I'll miss you when you've gone.' Which was at least partly true. He'd taken the cellar job so he could catch up on his studies between customers, but in the end some things were more interesting than textbooks.

The man wasn't listening. He was looking across at the beer drinker – who looked at his watch, emptied his glass, stood up, and went straight up the stairs to the hotel lobby, his phone held to his ear.

The barman remembered that there was no signal in the cellar.

The whisky drinker finished his drink as well. He contemplated the ice in the empty glass. The meltwater slowly accumulated at the bottom, the way it does at the base of a glacier in the spring.

At last he looked up. 'Well,' he said, 'there's nothing more I can do tonight. I'll be off. Good night.'

'Good*bye*, sir.'

'Goodbye.'

The next day was one of those days that clearly sort out who is who. The sun never really rose properly: instead, the village was full of cloud that got a little brighter when morning came, cloud laden with sticky heavy flakes of wet snow. The natives used the day to do their washing and ironing. Most of the visitors were sensible and got up late, had two-hour breakfasts, and sat indoors getting on each other's nerves. The gym was full, and the cinema arranged extra daytime showings.

But some people only had a week's holiday and they'd already paid for their lift passes. They sat around in the cafés in little eager groups, watching the cloud with constant hope – look, it's a bit brighter, the sun's burning through – yes, it is – no, it isn't – perhaps it's clear on top. In the late morning, a few people were seized with a vision of majestic peaks soaring into the sunshine above a broad smooth lake of cloud. The vision spread, and a general migration started towards the cable-car that went up to the edge of the glacier.

At the top lift station it was still foggy but at least the falling snow was drier. It came in tiny little hard pellets. Having come so far, you might as well go further, and a queue formed for the button-lift that went up and onto the glacier itself. There, surely, at last, would be the blue sky and the perfect fresh new snow of everyone's vision.

It was indeed a different world once the lift had dragged you out of the hollow and into the wind – but it was different in a different way. There was nothing. You held on to your button in dead silence, moving on nothing, surrounded by nothing. From time to time a black pylon would loom up out of the whiteness, shoot past you with a clang and a jerk that threatened to throw you off your skis, and vanish as quickly as it had come. Then there was nothing again. Nothing except the wind. It was strong and perfectly steady. It was perfectly cold, and relentless. It found every thin point, every gap, every half-open zip. It threw icy snow in your face that stung like salt. It made your eyes water and it made your body colder, steadily colder. People started to shout out loud to themselves, words, numbers, songs, anything to stay conscious and not fall off the lift and into the nothingness without end.

The endless nothingness ended. The white ground heaved up under everyone's skis and shot them one by one round the corner and within sight of a pole embedded in the snow. By the time the pole had been passed, another had started to appear in the distance; and, in due course, another. It was too cold to consult maps, but the poles were sure to lead one back down to the lift station and light, and sight, and warmth. If they didn't, if they led into a crevasse instead, that was too bad: there was nothing else to follow.

Down at the lift station, the restaurant began to fill up. Coffee with brandy in it, tea with schnapps in it, anything with anything in it that might make warmth seem at least possible again. People lingered to revive themselves. They also lingered to avoid the humiliation of arriving back in the village less than an hour after leaving it, and on the same cable car.

Perched on orange plastic chairs round a small table, three serious Bavarians in what looked like leather ski-suits were systematically drinking Jägermeister. Jägermeister is a worthy product of the land that gave us weltschmerz, schadenfreude, and angst. It tastes so vile that you have to down it in one. Like some Wagnerian magic weapon, it will heal any wounds except the ones it has caused itself – and the hangovers that Jägermeister causes are cosmic ones. Once it was drunk only by vagrants in doorways, but now it is served by blondes to black-clad graphic designers in crucially fashionable bars across the civilised world. As it happened, these Bavarians were not drinking Jägermeister ironically or post-modernly, they were drinking it because it was cheap. Anyway, it was something to do.

Across the room an irregular nebula had formed round one of the mountain rescue team, who had descended god-like from some remote Olympus and was permitting himself to be bought drinks. Like a girl in a brothel, what he was actually consuming was not alcohol but coloured water, for he was still technically on duty; but unlike the girl, he would have the real drinks to take home at the end of the day to share with his family and friends. This made the tribute a genuine gift, and he repaid it with stories – as is right, just as gods and heroes have done throughout the ages.

He told them of the glacier, how the lifts had to be realigned twice a year because of the moving ice. How the crevasses were carefully surveyed and carefully marked but how you should still never take your skis off when you were anywhere near one, in case your boots punched a hole in the snow cover and you fell into the void beneath. How if the glacier did take you, you would spend 10, 15, 20 years in its embrace until one summer they found you among the melting ice at the bottom and they took you and gave you a discreet and reverent burial in the churchyard. How the currents in the flowing ice would stretch you so that you might come out twice as tall as when you went in. How the town museum's historical collection had first refusal of any small things that survived the journey. Watches, compasses, altimeters: things like that.

Another apple juice and soda, and he told a stranger story. There were three people went out on the glacier once, in my grandfather's time. Two men and a woman – a couple, and a friend of theirs, that's how we saw it. That night, two people came back: one man and one woman. They were in shock. The other man had disappeared, they said, on the glacier. We wondered about that. Was it a love triangle? Did he fall? Did he jump? Did *she* push him? Did *he* push him?

The speaker paused. You see, he went on, he's never come out. Seventy years and no sign. The experts say he must be caught in some huge eddy, a whirlpool under the ice. Some huge eddy under the ice going round and round, deeper and deeper. Perhaps he'll come out in a thousand years, perhaps never.

Unseen, the red-haired man had come nearly to the centre of the group. Towards the end of the story, still unseen, he slipped out. That's the thing about not looking at yourself in the mirror. That's the thing about not looking at other people. In the end no-one looks at you. No-one saw him put his skis on and start towards where bright yellow signs in three languages warned of a run closed because of avalanche danger.

And no-one saw a tall figure detach itself from the shadows outside the lift station and start to follow him.

'As you pass the barrier and enter the path, the tunnel of steel that was crushing your chest unlocks and melts away.

You are in a tunnel of cloud now. It softly encloses the trees on one side and the rocks on the other. It's a new kind of tunnel that embraces you instead of strangling you. Travelling through it, you have as little freedom as a pinball; and as little anxiety. The final move has already been made, the final decision taken, the final run started. Whatever is going to happen is already going to happen. There is no more to be said.

'On the right, the rocks loom over the path: huge and dark, seemingly threatening but as innocent as the earth they come from. On the left, the nearest trees stand out greenish-black against the colourless grey cloud. Each tree is uniquely itself. Each rejoices in its tree-ness and selfness and its unchanging place on the mountain.

'You are skiing blindly in the fog and each corner might easily be your last, but each corner brings new visions of transcendence. Not only trees but bushes, boulders, even the snow – everything is in such an intense state of being that its joy would be intolerable if you were not already becoming part of it all yourself.

'The silence is so absolute that no sound is possible, but even the silence is no longer an absence of sound but some-thing positive and physical in its own right, and you breast through it like a swimmer.

'You have lost all desire for the end that you sought. You have lost all desire, full stop. That is good – but it will not last. When you come out of this cloud and back into the sharp-edged world the tunnel of steel will be waiting for you and it will start to close in again. Bit by bit, you will stop looking at yourself, and you will stop looking at other people. In the end you will stop looking when you cross the road; and this time I will not be there with you.

'So now into that white silence another thing comes. You perceive it first as a shadow in the corner of your eye, and then, coming up on your right, you see a figure on skis.

'It is I.

'I must look quaint to you. A quaint anachronism with my knickerbockers and stockings, with my long, long skis, the way I half kneel as I take each turn. We are taking the turns together now. I move up beside you and we look at each other for a moment. You look better than you did last night. You look free.

'I am glad but still I don't trust you. Still I have to make this permanent.

'You see me properly for the first time, a stranger bareheaded in the wind, someone unburdened by hat or goggles or gloves, someone unburdened by anything any more, someone your age or younger, as if the past seventy years had never been. Even if you had looked at me in the bar last night, you wouldn't recognise me today. Do you resent my presence in your private world? I think not. I think that you see me the way you see the trees: uniquely myself, something to be celebrated.

'It is time to take action. I can never undo what I did that day, but perhaps I can atone.

'It is time, now.

'I fall back a couple of feet and raise my left arm. I take careful aim. The first sound that this silent world has ever known is the sound of my ski pole smashing into your wrist and the clatter of your pole falling to the ground.

'You lurch from side to side as you shake your wrist to ease the pain, but you do not fall. A good skier can ski just as well with one pole or even none at all; and you are a good skier.

'In an instant, your state of contemplation has gone. Surprise comes, and anger ignites, and finally there comes rage, pure, burning rage. Surprise – obviously. Anger – the anger of someone distracted from his self-destructive course. And rage above all – rage at the absurdity of it, at how silly it is to be angry when someone threatens you with the annihilation you had already chosen for yourself. Pure rage, burning rage, cleansing rage, good rage – a flame that raises you to red heat and beyond, and incinerates your pain and your devils into ash. White ash, light ash for the breeze to blow away.

'I watch you from behind. I wait: timing is everything. I come up beside you again. You see that you are safe from my poles, because I am holding them in my right hand, on the side away from you. My empty left hand is next to yours. If we wanted, we could shake hands. I turn my face to you and open my mouth as if to say something. You lean towards me to hear, and we travel on like that for fifty, perhaps a hundred yards, and then the path turns sharply away to the right and we don't, and there is nothing under your skis any more.

'The next sound to come to the silent world is the sound of something breaking. Something that is not a branch. Then other sounds begin: I do not listen to them. There are a few things left to be done. I do those things, and I leave. At last it is over. For you, and, I hope, for me.'

The rules of the mountain rescue service lay down clearly what is to be recorded in its log. The purpose of a log is strictly factual. It exists to answer questions and not to raise them. Logs are meant for reading in brightly-lit offices and for filing away. The rules of the mountain rescue service make no mention of truth. The truth is not for writing down. The truth is for discussing and puzzling over at night over drinks in front of the embers of a dying wood fire.

Thus the log records the phone call that alerted the rescuers to the accident, but it says nothing of the voice that made the call. Calm and utterly precise, giving the details clearly at dictation speed, like an announcer from the early days of radio. Calm and precise and grammatical and yet, deep underneath (so the man who took the call told his friends) with a suppressed tone of exultation.

The log records that the victim was found exactly in the expected position and it precisely records the shattered state of his leg where it had hit the tree. It says nothing of the victim's own silver survival blanket, taken out of his backpack, carefully unfolded and tenderly tucked round him to keep him alive until the rescuers came. It mentions the finding of the mobile phone on which the emergency call was made, but not the fact that it was out of the reach of anyone who could have made the call.

It is the cheerful practice of the mountain rescue team to inject their clients with a nice big shot of something useful before strapping them to a stretcher and starting the journey to hospital. It makes things more pleasant for everyone. That year the mixture was unusually hallucinogenic. Sounds were seen, sights were heard, things imagined became things remembered and things remembered became things imagined until the brain lost patience and erased the lot. The one memory that survived was a sound. Out of the silence and the screaming, one voice, one word, one command.

At the end of the season, the barman remembered the bottle again and took it out of its hiding-place. It was empty except for a little sediment and a stale smell.

Summer came, and the town museum acquired some exceptionally old objects to add to its historical exhibits.

The skier's leg was full of metal but he had learnt to walk on it again. In a life full of many new realities, one strange memory remained. He could bring it back easily enough: among all the voicemails that had accumulated during his slow recovery, one short message was always there, resisting the attempts of the automatic systems to erase it. A voice clear and distant as if coming from beyond the stars, a tone of triumph and relief. One voice, one word, one command:

'Live.'

Gingerbread

Snow was falling on the crowds of people waiting for the train. It fell in flakes the size of prawn crackers, soggy heavy flakes that splashed when they hit you.

The station was crowded with wet people. Something had happened higher up the line, so that no-one from the other side of the ridge could get over it to get home. They had to take a train down, another one all the way round the base of the mountain, and yet another one to get back up again – a four-hour journey at least. I felt sorry for them in theory, but it was late on a grey afternoon and I wanted to get home and they were bleating around like sheep and getting in my way.

The crowd swirled a bit and I found myself mixed up in a bunch of damp Viking giants. A few minutes with my nose buried in their shoulder-blades and I decided that enough was enough. If I wanted to stand in a wet crowd waiting for non-existent transport, I had plenty of opportunities for doing it at home.

I pushed my way out of the station and put my skis back on. The run down would be unpleasant and wet but there was nothing really difficult about it – on a good day, it was over in a couple of minutes. I just had to go down between two outstretched fingers of the forest, and once they joined together, there was Reality Checkpoint and I'd soon be home and warm and eating cake.

The weather was the same as when I'd gone into the station, only more so. The light was greyer and the wet sticky flakes had merged into a morass like half-set cement. For slushhounds with short fat grungy skis it would have been perfect, but my skis were built for snow. In this stuff, they slowed to a sticky crawl. Every time I turned, it had to be with a yank and a jump and a squelch.

Trees usually give you some good shadows to see the bumps by, but now the light was flat even when I got near them – what light there was. There was no way to tell which way was down. A few times I got caught by invisible bumps that stopped my skis while my body tried to carry on. Then one of them grabbed me in mid-turn and gave my knee a wrench. I felt something give. 'We'd better get down before it stiffens up,' the voice said. It came from somewhere inside my head.

The snow was sticking to the trees as well as the ground. Once, a heavily laden branch dumped its whole load down my back, in the gap past my sodden scarf. 'He's getting wet,' said the voice. I struggled on.

Finally I fell completely, my skis splayed out and my feet firmly held in the bindings because the fall was too slow to make them let go. Every time I tried to get out of the situation, it seemed to stretch some part of my body that wasn't built to be stretchable. I paused for a rest. I was comfortable as long as I didn't move. I wasn't going to fall any further and I was happy where I was. Anyway, I deserved a rest. 'He's given up,' the voice said. Which didn't seem fair.

The automatic mechanical bit of my mind started tabulating facts. How long people survive when plunged into cold water. How it's easier to die of hypothermia when the temperature's above zero than it is when it's freezing but dry and you're losing fingers and toes to frostbite. I ignored the tabulation, much as I usually do. All in all I didn't mind dying, but it did seem unfair that someone else would get to eat our cake. I really resented that.

I lay quietly for a bit to fool my body into thinking I wasn't planning to move. It was comfortable where it was. If it thought I was going to stir it up, it would put thoughts into my mind to discourage me – I've lost whole gym sessions that way in the past. At a random moment, without notice, I leapt into action, not knowing what I was doing till I did it. With a poke of my pole I got one ski off, then I twisted round and removed the other. Soon I was standing with skis in one hand and poles in the other, looking round for inspiration. My blood was pumping and I felt shaky, but my mind was clear at last. The situation was dangerous. This really was an emergency. I had to do something decisive.

In the distance, I saw a faint light in the trees on the other side of the clearing. Light meant human activity of some kind. It had to be a house. A house meant warmth, safety, company. It *had* to be a house.

Whatever it was, it seemed to be a little below me, an easy traverse, but I didn't put my skis on. In my present state, if I misjudged the height and ended up a couple of yards below that light, that would be it. That would be where they'd find me in the morning.

The closer I got, the more like a house it looked. I got to the trees next to it and leant my skis there and carried on. Yes, the light came from a window, and next to it was a dark blank space that must be a door. I tapped on it but it made no sound. I banged hard, but the sound was dull like when you thump a tree. I didn't see how anyone could hear.

I waited. I got as far as deciding that I'd better take my boot off and smash the window with it – in an emergency, everything is permitted – and then the door opened and the light dazzled me.

I had to adjust my ideas rapidly because I'd somehow been expecting a large angry Swiss, but all there was between me and the light and warmth was a small woman who stood politely to one side and let me tumble in.

My next memories are rather confused. She was old as well as small, dressed in the softest grey, and her white hair was pulled away from her face and tied back with something and she had the most beautiful bones I have ever seen. She helped me to get my wet clothes off, and her English was as old and delicate as she was, as if it had been put away in a drawer with dried lavender to keep it fresh, and her name was Margaret.

I remember smelling the smell of coffee, and holding a big bowl of it in my hands. I remember sitting by the tall porcelain stove, wrapped in an enormous black cloak. I remember my socks hanging on the stove and giving off a reassuring smell of wet dog.

Margaret came in with a tray. If it had been cake then I'd have known that I was dead. But it was gingerbread. She held the tray and urged me to choose between gingerbread men, and ducks, and dogs. I picked up a duck, and hesitated.

She laughed. 'When I was a little girl,' she said, 'someone gave me one of those. I didn't know where to start. I thought and thought and I opened my mouth wide and bit off its head. Then I looked at what I'd done and I cried and cried, because I'd killed it.'

That was all she ever told me about herself. It didn't seem polite to ask her anything, not polite and not entirely safe – there was something magical about this place and I was afraid that if I said the wrong thing at the wrong moment it would all vanish and I'd be back outside in the snow.

But the gingerbread was so very, very good. She said she'd added cinnamon, that's what made it so special. As we ate, we talked. She wanted to know all about how I got there, and I told her. She told me she'd left the curtains open specially so I'd see the light, which sounded a bit backwards but I wasn't complaining. Somehow she got me telling her about the voice I'd heard and she told me it was perfectly normal. 'At the end of everything, when the cold comes, the silent part of your soul turns round and speaks words to you.' I remember wondering how she knew.

Then she asked how the skiing was and was I enjoying it, and what everyone's favourite bars were and everything. I began to feel a bit sorry for her stuck all the way out here in the wilderness with all these questions and no-one to ask, so I told her everything I could. I told her the story of Reality Checkpoint, because I thought it might make her laugh. She lived so close to it, she ought to know the place.

Of course Reality Checkpoint isn't its real name. Its real name is something Gothic that none of us has managed to read. But it's real enough and it brings you right down to earth after your day's skiing. The waitresses are beer-spilling blondes – stunners – but at the centre of it all sits that strange man Johann. He's old and bent and angry. Mostly when we see him it's because he's in a rage with someone. Often it's couples. One moment he's giving them romantic his'n'hers cocktails with day-glo plastic palm trees, the next he's yelling at them.

Charlotte says it's because he's bent in other ways than just his spine but then Charlotte says that sort of thing about everyone from Brad Pitt downwards. My guess is she was right once, a long time ago, so now she keeps saying it in case one day she's right again and everyone will tell her how clever she is again.

Anyway there's a sure test. I've watched his waitresses and they get more beautiful the longer they work for him. It's like when your friend gets a really dowdy new girlfriend and you wonder what he sees in her and she unfurls and blossoms under his care and you kick yourself for not having seen it first. No, Johann isn't gay, he's just strange. He works harder than anyone to make sure his guests have a really good time, and then for some reason he gets really unhappy when they do. Strange and sad. And I think he's older than we think.

His venom has pickled him and preserved him like a spider in a museum bottle.

I told Margaret a version of all this but all she said was 'Poor Johann,' very quietly. She didn't find it funny at all. She was a kind soul.

She went to the window and looked out into the night. She went to the stove and felt my clothes to see if they were dry yet. I took the opportunity to have a discreet look round me. Nothing that said anything much, but on a table there was a photograph in a silver frame, of a young man looking pleased in a tunic with big shiny buttons. Her son, perhaps? I glanced at her left hand – I'm always forgetting to do this and people laugh at me for it – but there was no wedding ring on it, just a plain ring with a reddish irregular-shaped stone held into place with silver wire.

She saw me looking. 'It's a carnelian,' she said, and smiled. 'Your clothes are dry enough, I think. The snow has stopped and the moon is bright. You will have an easy journey.'

We finished the last bits of gingerbread and she tactfully went off to the kitchen while I dressed.

'Philip, will you do something for me?' she asked as I was putting my boots on. 'Your way home lies past… "Reality Checkpoint." Will you go in, and ask Johann for something?'

I couldn't really say no – and after what I'd been through, I couldn't see how Johann could scare me any more.

'It's not a message, just – just ask him to give you a glass of Quittenwasser. Quittenwasser. It's a drink.' She repeated the name slowly and clearly. 'Quittenwasser. He will know what you mean. Will you ask him for it?'

She made me repeat the name back to her till she was satisfied I'd get it right. I asked her again if there was any message, but she said no. 'But if he asks you where you have come from, tell him everything he wants to know.'

There was nothing left for us to say to each other. After I'd put my boots on I tried to stammer some sort of thanks but she pulled my head down to her level and kissed my cheek, it felt as light and dry as a dead leaf. As I walked towards where I'd left my skis she called out to me one last time: 'Good night, Philip! Stay warm! And remember the Quittenwasser!'

The sky was clear now, and there was a frost. The snow was hard and crisp and the moon cast shadows in front of me. I could see where I was going. My legs felt fit and precise. I came to the place where Reality Checkpoint loomed over the path. It was dimly lit because it was late and everyone had gone home. I told myself I'd come up and see Johann tomorrow, but then I saw the light by the loos. Johann keeps them open all evening just in case, and it came to me that I'd been too shy at Margaret's, and I could really use the facilities just now.

As I was coming out, I saw a shadow pressed against the glass of the door to the bar. Johann, watching me. I couldn't put it off any more. I went up to the door and stood facing him. He said something hostile that I couldn't hear and waved his hands at me to tell me he was closed, go away. I didn't move. I stayed there. I leaned towards him and said 'Quittenwasser' – which of course he couldn't hear either.

He opened the door to tell me to go away, and I said 'Quittenwasser' again.

I've seen Johann explode before, but never so fast. He demanded to know who sent me to laugh at him and he began screaming at me, mostly in German. I didn't care. I waited impassively for him to finish. The shouting was nice. It reminded me I wasn't dead.

In the end he tired himself out and I chose my moment and I said 'Quittenwasser' one more time. I felt like the Creature from the Swamp in a B movie, with just one line to say over and over again.

Johann didn't re-explode. He scuttled away to the bar and dived behind it. I waited uncertainly. Perhaps he kept a hatchet there. But when I stepped in and closed the door behind me, he'd pulled out a table, set two chairs by it, and put out a bottle and a glass. I came and sat down, and he poured a little of the drink into the glass and stood over me, watching me.

It was sour beyond belief. My mouth twisted up at the taste. It still does now, when I think of it. I looked at Johann, puzzled. When he saw the puzzlement in my face, his hostility faded. 'Who told you about it?' he asked.

'Your neighbour,' I said. 'She told me.'

At this, Johann went back to the bar and reached for a bottle of Williams and two new glasses. It was the special schnapps with a preserved pear floating in it. He brought everything back to the table and sat down opposite me.

'Tell me everything,' he said, in a soft tone that was more disconcerting than all the rage.

So I told him what I could. He snorted derisively when I told him about deciding to ski down (he was right) but mostly he just listened and listened. Then he began to ask me questions about everything, more questions than I knew how to answer. How Margaret looked, what she was wearing, how the room was furnished...

It seemed strange to me that he hadn't been to her house. Perhaps these two old people had quarrelled. Johann seemed more human in this dim light, but he was still a strange man after all.

He'd finished taking me through everything in the room for a second time – it didn't add much, I'd make a lousy detective – and suddenly I remembered the photograph of the young man in buttons and told Johann about it.

'So,' he said. Just that, 'So.' He hadn't really touched his schnapps before, but now he drained it and poured himself another glass.

'You are not the first person she sent to me, I think. The others delayed. Or they were frightened.' He gave a vulnerable smile. It looked alien on that sour face. And then he began to talk.

'We were young and in love.' He looked suspiciously at me, but no way was I going to laugh at anything he said.

'We were young, we were stupid. The war was coming.

'Her parents didn't like me, but she found an old shed up in the woods and that's where we'd meet. She made it pretty with flowers. She hung up one of her old smocks for a curtain. It was our own little home and we'd lie there for hours making plans.

'Plans! With a war coming.

'She'd bring food up for us to eat and in the autumn she made us a special schnapps out of quinces. Quittenwasser. It tasted horrible, but she said there was nothing wrong with it, it was too young and we should keep it for a few years.

'She'd wait for me there or I'd wait for her. We were Hansel and Gretel lost in the woods. I used to hug her close to keep her safe from bears.'

He managed to combine nostalgia with contempt. I didn't feel like laughing now, only crying.

'We were stupid. And then the war came.

'This country wasn't strong the way it is now. It was weak. Weak. We'd seen how Austria had gone. The Nazis could have walked in any time they wanted and taken over. They even had a timetable for it. A Swiss timetable.' A sour smile.

'It was a dangerous time. There were big lists everywhere to say who had to do what. I had to learn how to shoot. *She* said it was good because now the bears couldn't come to eat us up. Poor child.

'Suddenly in August they sent for me. I was wanted. I had to go at once, just on the train and go. I was being sent to Germany. To a sawmill near Freiburg. I'd be an ordinary German. I'd see how they worked – what they felt – what they thought – what they ate – I'd report it all back to people who would understand it. It was one little piece of the picture, but if it was good, my report might go all the way up to the General himself.

'I saw him just once, for a minute or two. I was in my German clothes already and he spoke to me and I replied in my German accent. "No job is too small," he told me. "All of them have to be done if we are to live."

'The General was our dictator, did you know? We appointed him and he was our whole government until the war ended. Then he went home. When he died in 1960 he was an ordinary private citizen. He had a private funeral. Nobody said anything but we all knew. A quarter of a million of us went to it. We went as private citizens, that was all. We went because he was our General and he saved us.

'When I got to Freiburg, something had gone wrong. My contact wasn't there. I went ahead and took the job anyway. What else could I do? I was there four years. Then things were ending and no-one cared much about borders any more. I came back here. Everything bad had ended. I was Swiss again. I could see my Gretel again.

'She wasn't there. Her family wouldn't speak to me. I went up to our little house to see if she'd left a note in our secret place – where I'd promised to leave a note for her, only there was no time and I wasn't allowed. The roof was rotted and falling in. Flowers were growing on the earth inside. Beautiful flowers. In the secret place there was nothing.

'Later, little by little, I heard from people what had happened. She'd carried on visiting our little house all that summer and autumn. She'd wait all day for me to come. The days got shorter and colder. One day she caught a chill, and they couldn't do anything for her. It was wartime, you see.

'After I'd heard that, I went back up to the ruined house and in the secret place I left her the ring I'd got her in Germany. It had cost me three days without food to buy it. Have *you* ever been hungry for three days? It was a red ring in a silver setting.'

'Reddish orange,' I said. 'With twisted silver wire. I've remembered it now.' I swear until that moment I'd forgotten it. Absurdly, we said the next words together. 'A carnelian.'

'So.' There was a silence. He looked tired.

When he spoke in the end, he was different. He wasn't in the past any more. His voice was clear and firm. 'There is much to do.'

I ought to say that this is my last memory of Johann, sitting at the table with the Williams bottle in front of him, making his plans; but in fact he gave me a lift to town in his 4x4. So there was no proper final farewell scene.

The next few days I spent skiing on the Mürren side, where the landscape looks like the moon and there's a revolving restaurant on top of a mountain, James Bond style. I forgot about Johann and everything, until I was watching the snow reports over breakfast one morning. A news item said that the missing owner of Reality Checkpoint had been found after a big search, up by a ruined shack in the woods. He was frozen stiff, and on his finger was a ring no-one had seen before. A reddish stone wrapped in silver wire. A carnelian.

A quarter of a million people did not go to his funeral. But I did.

Miss Poyser

The spindly armchair was made of wood. It had a hard satin pad on the seat and another round hard pad on the back, that stuck into your back if you slumped. Miss Poyser approved. Miss Poyser never slumped. 'Poyser by name, poised by nature,' they'd said when she was younger, and she saw no reason to start sagging just because she was old.

When you have taken a house for the season, even if it is a tiny house in the street next to the post office, it is polite to pay a call on your next-door neighbour. Miss Poyser approved of politeness. In any case, it was practical: it would have been silly to spend week after week ignoring each other on the street and in the shops. Politeness was often practical.

Miss Poyser and her hostess sat on two chairs turned at an angle towards the window and the glass-panelled door that led from the porch. If the street had been less steep, one would have seen the shapes of the passers-by whose voices came in only as a murmur through the window, triple-glazed against the cold. If the front door had been open, the daylight would have shone in and been broken up into bulbous deep-sea shapes by the irregular glass panels of the inner door.

Her hostess was older than Miss Poyser, a little bent with age, indeed; but her straight iron-grey hair gave her a certain dignity very different from her guest's ebullient snow-white curls. Miss Poyser had accepted a second one of the hard, aromatic biscuits that her hostess had baked, but declined a third. The coffee was good and strong and served in tiny cups, so that it was possible to accept a second cup without risk to her heart. Miss Poyser approved of this. If guests were thirsty then they should drink before they came, good fresh water in a nice big glass. The purpose of a visit was companionship, not gross feeding and drinking.

The afternoon light had faded into dusk, and the conversation had faded away with it. Miss Poyser approved of this also. She considered it morbid to maintain a ceaseless flow of chatter for the sake of chatter. She had recently instituted quiet periods in her school, to teach the children not to be afraid of silence when silence was right. They might spend the rest of their lives plugged into headphones, conceivably they might, but at least she would have done what she could.

A fragile Louis XVI-style clock tinkled four times, bloodlessly. The silence became watchful. Miss Poyser began to feel *de trop*, as if her hostess were waiting for something and wanted to encounter it on her own. But Miss Poyser made no move to leave. She could be remarkably obtuse when obtuseness was what was called for.

The front-door handle rattled, and the door must have opened, because patterns of light writhed in the glass panels of the inner door. The sound of cheerful footsteps, the clatter of skis being put down and boots taken off, and something like a laugh.

There was nothing more. Just when one might have expected someone to turn the handle of the inner door and open it, the sounds faded, the silence returned, and the light vanished from the glass.

Miss Poyser put her coffee-cup precisely and silently down onto its saucer.

'Did you see?' her hostess asked. 'Did you hear?'

'I saw,' Miss Poyser replied.

'What did you see?'

'I saw.'

A pause.

'You were not here the day the cable broke.'

'No,' said Miss Poyser quietly. 'I was not there when the cable broke.' She sounded like a language lesson, repeating phrases.

'Perhaps they will come in – tomorrow.' Her hostess seemed to be talking to herself.

Miss Poyser counted silently to thirteen. 'What will you tell them?' There was no answer. She counted her heart-beats again. 'What will you tell them?'

Her hostess was sitting rigidly upright. 'That I waited. That I did not forget.' There was stubborn tearful pride in her voice.

Miss Poyser thought for a while.

'The children cried when I went away,' she said. 'I know they haven't forgotten but I hope they're not *waiting*.

'I want them to run about and shout and fall over and get up and run about again.

'I want them to make drawings and say, "that was pretty, I'll keep it to show Miss Poyser." I want them to have adventures and say, "that was exciting, I'll remember it to tell Miss Poyser."

'I don't want faithfulness, I want *stories.*'

Miss Poyser took a deep breath. Her voice was poised and steady. 'That's why I go on. To have something to tell. When they come.' She was talking about a different 'they,' now.

'You are waiting also?'

'One should not merely wait.'

'Perhaps tomorrow – '

'My dear friend, I must not be rude, but you are *young.* They will not come for you tomorrow.

'And if they do come unexpectedly when you are not here, do you think they'll go away again? Be sure that when they come for you they will find you, wherever in the wide world you are. Do you think they love you so little, that they wouldn't do that?'

'Tomorrow – '

'Tomorrow, my dear, you shall not make your fragrant cakes simply to be crumbs for the birds. Tomorrow we will set out to find stories.'

'Where? There are no stories now.'

'We shall go to Peliti's. There is a new kind of cake there. They call it Tropical Forest. It is like a Black Forest cake, but with molasses. Everyone is waiting to know what you think of it. They want to hear what you will have to say. It will make a silly, small story, but it is a start.'

Her hostess had turned to look at her. 'Peliti's?' she said haughtily. 'Who baked it?'

'Gianmarco'.

'Marco.' There was an obscure gleam in the deep-set eyes. 'Then it will be hopeless.'

Miss Poyser rose from the chair and swept non-existent crumbs from her lap.

'Until tomorrow, then.'

'Until tomorrow, Miss Poyser. But really, the boy cannot cook anything!'

I know, thought Miss Poyser as she walked to the door. *That's why I asked him to do it.*

In the porch there were lumps of snow that certainly hadn't been there when Miss Poyser came in.

They might come sooner than expected, after all.

Still, whenever they came, they would have stories.

84

Downhill

You're a chameleon, Victoria told me last night at dinner. It's the sort of thing she says. Put you next to someone, she said, and you take on their colour in no time. You just become like whoever you're with.

That could have been an epigram, or a criticism. Being Victoria, probably a bit of both. Like when she told me that my girlfriend liked being taken out to Japanese restaurants only because they were very expensive and gave you nothing to eat. It was too good not to repeat, but it was toxic if you did. I found that out to my cost.

The thing about Victoria is that she views every relationship as a continuation of war by other means. Sex and power are the same thing, for her. When we were at university together I discovered this just in time – only just, in fact. Going to bed with Victoria is just like going to bed with a man, they used to say. And that's an epigram too.

Being on a skiing holiday with my two best friends is a pretty good test of Victoria's chameleon theory. Can I be a calculating over-educated intellectual like Victoria and simultaneously an impulsive carefree meathead like Charlie? Actually, I think I can. Put a chameleon on a tartan rug and it'll have a nervous breakdown, but I rather enjoy the experience. It's good to be stretched.

Today was definitely a tartan sort of day, in chameleon terms. It started Charlie-coloured, because we went to the ski shop together to see about hiring some snowboards for tomorrow. Try everything once, that's Charlie and me. Now the man at the ski shop was from New Zealand, and when someone from Nizullund talks about sex, he calls it 'six.' The guy in the shop didn't talk about sex at all, but it being snow-boards, he had to talk about decks rather a lot. Charlie was enchanted, and if he was, I was.

To add to Victoria's irritation, our deck-sounds-like-dick jokes don't all come out at once (so to speak). We got size and stiffness out of the way very quickly, and even colour and shape only lasted us till half-way up the first lift. We honestly did mean to be grown up and serious after that, but a couple of runs later we saw a group of snowboarders and realised, quite independently, in a grown-up and serious way, that some of liked to rard their dicks one way round and some the other. It was hard luck on Victoria that she was sitting between us on the chairlift at the time. 'Can I ride yours if I let you have a go on mine?' And so on.

Victoria never counter-attacks frontally, because that would be no fun. On the cable car up to lunch she merely started thinking aloud about the Roman legions and how far they had got into the Tyrol. I'm sure she gets these things from reading the back covers of serious paperbacks, but that doesn't stop them being interesting. By the time she'd mixed in Hannibal (but everyone knows he crossed the Alps over the St Bernard, not here) it was too fascinating for me not to join in. I knew nothing about the subject, but then talking about things you already know about it is just *dull*.

The only minor drawback from Victoria's point of view was that Charlie didn't mind us talking over his head at all. Charlie never minds – that's Charlie. At lunch, sitting on benches at the long table, beer-hall style, he embedded himself happily in soup and chips while Victoria and I carried on into the Roman provinces of Dacia, Moesia, Upper and Lower Pannonia, and other places I've forgotten. I have no idea where they all are. That's what makes it such fun.

Long scrubbed tables mean neighbours, and long wooden benches mean that you notice them when they try to get in or out. Sort of breaking the ice by breaking the shins. I said that, not Victoria. I can do epigrams too.

Our new neighbour apologized. 'Next time I'll try jumping in with both feet at once.'

'You'll slide all the way in.'

'No, my chin will stop me,' he said. He punched his jaw shut with his fist, to demonstrate. 'Sorry again.'

His name was Nicholas and he was from Holland.

It was Victoria who made the first move.

'The Flying Dutchman,' she said. Subtle, as ever. Then she had to add: 'No, Charlie, not a train, the Flying *Scotsman* is a train, the Flying Dutchman is an *opera*.' Opera is something Victoria knows about, because opera is something powerful people go to.

'The legend is older than the opera,' said Nicholas, not overawed in the least. 'Besides, you can never trust Wagner.'

'Why not?' Victoria sounded disapproving and condescending at the same time. Wagner is opera, and opera is something that powerful people...

'Well, look at it. Cursed and condemned to sail the seven seas forever, it could happen to anyone, I guess. Allowed on shore once a year – or is it seven years? – to look for love, I'll allow that, you need the girl or you haven't got your story. But all this business of dying for love? Come on! It's like *Tristan and Isolde*. You know, when they meet and fall in love? Remember? "Isolde, I love you." – "Tristan, I love you" – "Oh goody, let's drink poison together."' Nicholas raised his glass to emphasize the point. 'And anyway we're not on the ocean.'

'But snow *is* frozen water,' said Victoria.

'And in the summer I *do* sail,' Nicholas added, sabotaging his own argument with a grin.

It rather looked as if he was going to be skiing with us today. That wouldn't be a bad thing. Skiing with Victoria is *nothing like* skiing with a man. Take yesterday, for instance, behind the Dachstein glacier, 'a perfectly ravishing run' the guidebook says (I love those translations). Victoria fell early on, and so of course she got all shook up and so of course both of us had to stay with her. Because if one of us went off to ski the ravishing run leaving the other to stand guard, that would be admitting that looking after her was a duty instead of being the sole aim and fulfilment of our lives. So we both stayed with her until she got herself together, and then we escorted her down. We did our duty as gentlemen, but we were both savage as hell by the time we got home.

Having Nicholas with us could solve everything, really. We'd be three men, so one could squire and two could ravish – especially if Nicholas was happy to do the squiring. I got out the piste map and started talking in a general way about our plans for the afternoon.

'Where do you want to go?' Nicholas asked.

I pointed out a few possible routes that we'd thought of, and explained the problem about varying degrees of compet… er, *confidence*. Tact, you see. That's me.

'I know a route,' said Nicholas. 'It can be as long and hard as you like,' he said to Charlie, who luckily forgot to think of a deck joke in time. To me he said, 'There's always a gentler way round. We can do those parts separately and meet up again afterwards,' as if it was me he was being kind to. He gave a shy almost-smile to Victoria.

It sounded great. Nicholas and Victoria doing the cruising, Charlie and me on the chewy bits. So we went for it.

Getting up from the table, Charlie tipped his bench over. It had to happen to someone. It made a lovely crash.

Nicholas took us to a part of the mountain I didn't know; and I thought I knew them all. The paths through the trees split, and crossed, and merged, so you really needed to be sure where you were going. Perhaps that was why there was no-one on it now. If I'd been in charge then I'd have been worrying already, perhaps there's just one lift out of there, at the bottom, perhaps the lift man only works half-days: but Nicholas was pistemaster now and I just lay back and enjoyed being a passenger.

We were following a broad clearing straight down the hill. As it started to get narrower and a little steeper, Nicholas pointed out a horizontal-looking path off to the left. He said it was a road the foresters use in the summer. 'The next part is rather technical,' he said. 'We'll go round by the path and meet you at the bottom.' He went off with Victoria, leaving Charlie and me to do the interesting stuff.

'Technical' was right. The gap between the trees narrowed down until we found ourselves in a steep gully with knee-high bumps. You need skill for those. The key is not to go over the top of them, but almost. Then your skis have only one point of contact and it's easy to pivot them and sideslip down the far side. Technical, as Nicholas said; and beautiful too, if it's done properly, the way I do.

After I'd crossed the slope a couple of times I glanced back up to see how Charlie was doing: if he was about to come flying into me, I wanted notice of the fact. I needn't have worried. He was flowing across the snow with the ease of a natural dancer on his fourth day on skis, who has no idea yet what's meant to be difficult and what isn't. Ignorance protects you from fear.

My skis noticed me looking up, and being good skis, they obeyed. Before I could tell them they were wrong, I found myself down in the furrow between the bottoms of the moguls, locked into a nutter's groove that pointed downhill along a steep, straight diagonal. It's like when you're riding your bike on your friend's lawn and someone's left the hose out. Once your front wheel hits it, it holds on to the hose and it can't let go. It follows it wherever it's going – usually into the pond.

This groove was seriously nuts. It slashed across the slope straight towards a pine tree that stuck out from the others, perfectly placed for an instant gender change.

I'm not a fan of changing genders and I detest being stuck in a groove, nutter's or not, but my opinion didn't count for much just then. My skis were on opposite sides of the furrow, so they responded to opposite sets of bumps. First one knee tried to knock my teeth out and then the other one did – a crash course in spinal flexibility. Finally, at the very last bump, both my feet got thrown into the air at the same time, and me with them, and I twisted round somehow and scraped down the back of the icy mogul like a cat sliding down a corrugated iron roof. Then I was shooting back across the smooth snow at the bottom at a speed considerably exceeding v_{max}, until a friendly snowdrift stopped my skis dead.

I slid backwards out of the snowdrift and tried to look as if I'd planned the whole thing. I looked up to see how Charlie was getting on.

Charlie was gazing down at me and laughing loud enough to set off avalanches in neighbouring valleys. It was roll-around-on-the-floor laughing, but he was doing it on skis.

Roll-down-the-piste laughing, in fact.

It was epic to watch. If only I'd had a camera, I could have set it to music and got a million hits on YouTube. First Charlie bounced a few times, then he settled down to a nice steady freefall dive. Head first, skis last, because your skis are the biggest bit of you and they pick up the most drag from the snow. I did say that Charlie likes to throw himself into things head first. Well, he really does.

One other thing about Charlie: apart from hair gel and goggles, the only thing he wears when skiing is a ski suit open to the waist. He says he'd get too hot if he wore anything under it. That lacks class; but when you're in freefall down the mountain, an open ski suit makes a very good extra parachute. It slows you down by scooping up snow.

And *then* you stand up.

I didn't laugh. I thought it would twist the knife better if I didn't. I didn't even watch Charlie living through the severest case of snow balls I've seen. I looked away. A lens had come out of his goggles, so I went and picked it up and gave it back to him.

Just then, Nicholas and Victoria appeared, so Charlie put the goggles and the lens in his pocket for mending at the next lift. Victoria was crushingly sympathetic to poor Charlie. Once my loyal friend had told her all the earlier events that she'd missed seeing, she was equally gracious to me. We both felt honoured.

The next time we did that gully, we took extra care to do it perfectly. The key is to have two brains. One deals with the turn you're doing now, while the other looks ahead and plans where and when to do the next one. Some video games are like that – you launch your fingers and they get on with it while your brain plans the next action. Drinks parties are like that too, if you're Victoria, having one conversation while planning who to have the next one with.

The key is to have *only* two brains, not a third one that says 'Hold on, what if you fall?' Just go for it. So that's what I did. All the way down I was making short tight turns, so that my speed would never build up too much, and it worked. At the bottom, I was euphoric. I looked at my watch and counted my pulse: 137 beats per minute. Sixty seconds later it was already down to 104: that's what comes of being fit.

Nicholas and Victoria were being slower this time; or perhaps we'd been unusually fast. Charlie and I sat on the ground and shared an orange while we waited for them. Charlie lives on oranges. He buries the peel in the snow – says it's biodegradable. I disapprove of that, but not too loudly. I don't want sticky pockets any more than he does.

Charlie's goggles were still broken. I asked had he forgotten to mend them when we were going up the lift, and Charlie said there hadn't been a lift yet. I said yes there had, and I described it to him in exact detail. Yes, he said, but that was this morning, before lunch, didn't I remember? I didn't, as it happened, but neither lifts nor goggles seemed worth having an argument about.

Nicholas and Victoria came into view in the distance. She was sailing down, looking more relaxed than usual. Not dynamic, of course, but not creased up in her usual panic either. Stately, you could say. Nicholas was a little behind her, but not too far away to keep an eye on where she was going. Definitely she was skiing better. He didn't look bored.

It looked as if he was going to carry on looking after her. This was turning into rather a nice afternoon. I felt I could ski like this for ever.

Now that Charlie and I had showed what we could do if we liked, we stayed together with the others. It was nice, broad, flattering skiing. Nicholas skied next to Victoria while Charlie and I played around them. At some point I thought the burden should be shared and I asked Nicholas whether he wasn't bored with this simple stuff, but he just said, 'In my flat country, winter sports mean sleighs drawn by bicycles. After that, anything is steep.' It was so elegantly put, I didn't care whether it was true. I left them to it. Victoria was forgetting to talk about ancient Roman tribes, or even about the important people she knew. She sounded like an ordinary person, really. She could apply to re-join the human race, if only we could find the forms.

I held back for a bit to let the others get ahead, so I could pick up speed and get a proper gallop. There's something about going that fast when you're that close to the ground. It doubles the speed somehow. The tiniest bump becomes a major landmark. Things happen before you have time to think. You have to be 100% alert the whole time – it's a different kind of living. As I passed the others, I bled off a little speed by using my edges. It sounded like the thrusters on a spaceship making a mid-course correction. I did the same thing again a couple of times, then I started to slow down seriously, switching from edge to edge and throwing up great plumes of snow on either side. Finally, near the junction with another clearing, I put on the brakes and skidded sideways to a halt.

I looked down at where I'd kicked the snow away. Something lay there, something that someone had hidden under the snow earlier on.

Orange peel.

I looked up at the clearing that was coming down to join our path. I remembered it well. It was our gully. I remembered looking up there before, waiting for Charlie to come down.

This time I was certain. I'd been watching out for lifts, and there hadn't been one since the last time we'd been here. I was sure. We'd come here without a single lift, downhill all the way.

I stood in the hazy sunshine. The weather had been like this all afternoon. It should have given me sunburn by now. It hadn't. How long had we been out? I pushed back my cuff and looked at my watch. It said 3.15. That seemed reasonable, except that last time I'd looked at it, when I'd been measuring my pulse, it had also said 3.15. I looked at the second hand. It was still going round. The watch hadn't stopped.

I pressed down on the snow and it yielded just a tiny bit. It was still perfect. It should have been getting softer with time, but it hadn't.

Nicholas and Victoria came into view in the distance, just as they had before. Charlie was with them.

I ignored Charlie. I could see he was on one of his endorphin highs. You could tell him the world was ending, if you wanted, and he'd just say 'Hey, cool, let's go for it.' I caught Nicholas's eye. He looked guilty and vulnerable, all at once. That made sense. He was the one who had brought us here. This was *his* place. It had to be him.

We let the others carry on down the path. We looked at each other.

'I'm sorry,' Nicholas said eventually. 'If you've got only one day to find happiness, you can't help wanting to make the day longer.'

He waited for me to answer. I said nothing. It was more than I could digest all at once. He turned and skied down to join the others. I followed, at a distance.

They certainly made a nice couple, Nicholas and Victoria. The fact she wasn't trying to manipulate him was unique in history. You could see from their skiing how comfortable they felt together. They looked as if they'd known each other in another life.

At a bend in the path everyone paused to let me catch up.

Victoria looked at me and smiled. It was a happy, human smile. Nicholas had uncovered a Victoria I hadn't known existed. It happens sometimes – once you see something in a girl, everyone else starts to see it too. It's the mirror image of beginning to see some good in Japanese restaurants.

Or perhaps it was more than that, and he'd actually brought her to life just by being with her for a few hours.

It seemed a bit unfair but it didn't matter, really, because I still had one advantage over Nicholas. I know what the real Victoria is like. I've known her a long time and I know what makes her tick.

'Victoria,' I said, 'the committee meeting, isn't it today?'

It's all about power, you see. It's all about power.

Somewhere in the infinitely tedious politics of where Victoria works, there's a committee she isn't a member of. She has allies on it, and spies, but she isn't a member. It was due to meet today. Its decisions could affect the status of a project, one person's future, another person's standing... as I said, it's tedious. Since meeting her in the departure lounge at the airport, I'd heard the whole story from her three times, and listened to it once.

'The committee meeting,' I said, and sat back and waited for it to take effect. I knew it would work. It did. I saw it working. Nicholas saw it too.

'Darling,' Victoria said – to him, not to me, 'darling, I need to keep my finger on what's going on. I need to be available. Could we – ? Could I – ?' Un-Victoria-like hesitation. 'Can we see each other tomorrow?'

When you're on the top of the mountain and the guide says don't shout, and you *do* shout, and nothing happens, not to you – but you look down and you watch the white mountainside slip down and cover all the houses – that's what it felt like, what I'd just done.

Nicholas couldn't say that Victoria would be able to ski for hours yet and still not be late, without revealing his whole plan. Would that break the magic? Maybe it was just against the rules. Besides, whatever he said, Victoria wouldn't listen to him now. Her eyes weren't soft and blurry any more. I could see the cogs inside her head begin to revolve.

Nicholas looked down on her. He shook his head gently and said a word that, if it had come out without choking, would have been 'No.' Victoria looked up – not at Nicholas, her friend and on the way to being something more than a friend, but at an inconvenient datum, a minor obstacle to the grand strategy.

There was nothing more to be said. We skied on. At a given point Nicholas stopped, and so did we. 'The lift is over there to the right,' he said. 'I go this way.' He said goodbye to each of us in turn. He held Victoria's hands for a long time. She let him, politely. I couldn't bear to look at his face, so we hugged each other with averted eyes. Nicholas waved to Charlie and Charlie waved back. He wasn't eating an orange, so something of what had just happened must have got through even to him.

Just before the next bend in the path, Nicholas turned to wave to us. He wobbled, recovered, and then he was gone. We stood there for a bit. After a while, somewhere off to the right, we slowly began to hear the sound of the lift.

Back in the chalet, we're at the dinner table and we've just finished the main course. I stopped off at the jewellers on the way in, looking for expensive gifts for an expensive woman, but I couldn't see anything I could be sure of. It'll have to be an Hermès scarf at the airport again, a cliché but safe.

Charlie is in the kitchen, helping the chalet girl be very late with the pudding. Charlie does throw himself into things rather. I don't know if going to bed with Charlie is just like going to bed with a man, but I expect it will be. I hope they'll be happy.

Victoria is impressing herself and irritating our fellow guests by sending and receiving emails at the table. She's completely back to normal now. That has to be good. I suppose it must be. Normal, the way she's always been.

I wish I could undo what I did.

'In the summer, I sail,' he told us when we first met him.

This summer, we're going sailing. The sea is huge; but I don't care.

We're going to sail.

Cold Preserves

The knife is sharp. It's *sharp*. You can hold it next to your ear and hear its sharpness. It's so sharp you can cut yourself just thinking about it. Carlos is good at knives.

The square packet on the draining board is oozing blood. It trickles down in a thin line and makes fantastic patterns in the water at the bottom of the sink.

It's good to be doing this properly at last. I've been waiting a long time and now I'm about to do it. I was stupid not to have thought of it before. Such a lot of people had to give me ideas. Valerie and Carlos and even – God help us, even Mrs Ashbrook-Pembleton-French.

It all sounded so good at the beginning. We fought like cats to get here. The hottest resort in the brochure, the highest, the most expensive. The snow like cocaine, the air like champagne. The après-ski women wrapped head to foot in mink. The coolest ski bums in the Alps. In a word, quality.

And in the top resort, the top chalet. This one. Rare exotic woods that smell of honey. A wall of glass looking across the valley towards the sunset. Two saunas. Unlimited free drinks before dinner. In a word, *quality*.

Quality. Quality. And... a catering budget that would shame a prep school. Or a prison. The whole magical experience jeopardised by some bean-counter back in London whose mother brought him up on Wall's sausages.

The boss had the decency to sound embarrassed. 'Sorry, Fee, fuel costs have gone up so everyone's budget has to take a hit. You're clever, Fee, you're a genius, Fee, you'll cope.' So of course I cope. I'm clever. Osso buco. Belly of pork. Cuts of meat I'm ashamed to be seen buying: I tell the butcher they're for my dog. Braised gristle and boiled gristle and after five hours of slow cooking there's a smell in the kitchen like a glue factory. I disguise it with spices and the guests are all grateful and yes I'm a genius but it's heart-breaking because I know what I could really do for them if only I could. Five weeks I've been here, five *weeks*, and not one simple honest rump steak in all that time.

So now I'm unwrapping the bloody packet. A kilo, a glorious kilo of fillet. My knife floats through it soundlessly like a ski through powder. I make the slices. Regular. Even. Parallel. Perfect. Organic, grass-fed fillet steak, hung for twenty-one days, half my week's budget gone on a single piece of meat. The butcher was shocked, I saw the look he gave me. *She's mad*. That's what he was thinking.

I'm not mad. I love to make people happy, that's the thing. It doesn't matter if I'm cooking for a friend's dinner party, or catering a deer-stalking week in Scotland, or doing this. I like to take people out of the dreary microwaved existence of the rest of their grey little lives. I like to show them a bit of magic. I like to show them how things can be.

I like to enchant them till the week they've spent with me seems like the only real life and the other fifty-one weeks they have to crawl through are just... a parenthesis.

'We aim to give our guests an experience they will remember for the rest of their lives.' They said it on the web site. They said it in the brochure. That's why I applied. They said it at the final interview, when we had to cook a demonstration meal for them (there was no word of budgets, then). Their aim is my aim, that's why I fought for this job. That's why I put salt in my best friend's orange and Grand Marnier soufflé when she wasn't looking – because I like making people happy. That's why I've suffered so terribly all these weeks. That's why I'm ecstatic that at last I can serve our guests a dinner they'll remember for the rest of their lives. I can guarantee it. The rest of their lives.

I taste the Jerusalem artichoke soup. It's a symphony. I put it to one side to cool. At the last minute I'll heat it up and put the scallops into it, just long enough so they're delicately set like the white of a soft-boiled egg. One scallop per person. They're a pound each up here – no wonder, think how far from the sea we are – but happily there's no need to count. Not tonight.

Venetia says I'm middle-class.

On days when we've finished our chores early we all get together on Venetia's balcony to sunbathe. Venetia says I'm middle-class, the way I moan about money the whole time. I say it's all right for her, she had a party of lesbian vegans for a fortnight and now she's going to be in surplus the whole season. Venetia pushes her hair back and rolls her eyes and we both look at Val and we both remember Val's having it off with the butcher on a regular basis which means she has no problem with her budget and we both say nothing except Venetia, and Venetia says, 'And how *is* the butcher's meat, Valerie dear?' and we have to change the subject rather quickly so no-one says the word 'hung.'

Only we can't change it, really, and I find myself whining again that the guests eat everything I give them, there are no leftover scraps left to freeze and make that final-night they'll-be-too-drunk-to-notice isn't-she-clever budget-balancing saves-one's-bacon press-of-a-Magimix terrine. Val looks a bit bored by this and she says, she says to me if I'm really stuck there's always ways, and she recites this little verse:

> There was an old man of Zermatt
> Who was really exceedingly fat.
>> Because we were thinner,
>> We had him for dinner.
> Now what could be nicer than that?

'Don't be silly, dear,' says Venetia, 'Fee's oven is much too small, he wouldn't fit. Now then, everyone move round.' Venetia's determined to come home with an even tan. Fair's fair, it's her balcony.

Yes, my oven's small, but it's more than just that. I *love* my guests and I'll do anything to make them happy even if I suffer for it.

Take that Mrs Ashbrook-Pembleton-French. She came in my very first week when I was all new and excited. Her and her small son William, who's dyslexic or hyperactive or

103

ADHD or something. A menace, whatever. No, I remember, it was dyspraxic, because I remember wondering if I should tell her that dyspraxia might still do it in parts of Chelsea but all the best people's children in Notting Hill are pre-diabetic now. Kinder not to in the end, I thought, she's invested so much in it. So when he filled everyone's boots with snow I agreed with her that he couldn't help it, poor mite. And when she gave me a jar of William's special jam, all fruit no sugar and it grows whiskers if you don't keep it cold, I squeezed it into my fridge somehow (a chalet fridge is never empty) and I put some of my own things outside on the window-sill and if I got my fingers numb, well, I got a warm glow at the same time. As they say: cold hands, warm heart.

At the end of that first week they all said thank you and signed my visitors' book and when I'd changed the beds and put the bedclothes on to wash I sat down and read what they'd all written. And there it was, in the middle of the page, in big round illiterate ballpoint handwriting. There it was. Just two words. Two words for all my labour:

COLD PRESERVES

And that was that. Apparently I *hadn't warmed up the jam enough* before giving it to the dear dyspraxic darling and his teeth got all chilled.

I'd have cut the page out neatly and started again, only the same page had an adoring eulogy from David the shy actuary. It was almost a proposal of marriage, really, and that was so sweet because he'd spent all week staring at his shoes whenever I was near, I don't believe he even knew what I looked like. Anyway once I thought about it maturely I thought that Mrs A-P-F had damned herself more than she'd embarrassed me. Those big round wobbly letters like a retarded schoolgirl. That word 'preserves.' God help us, she probably has a couch at home instead of a sofa! And serviettes.

Damn, I've cut the last slice crooked. It's my fault for thinking daggers about the A-P-F. That slice'll have to be for me, then.

No, I love my guests. I respect them. They work hard and they struggle and save up and they come here to have something special in their lives and I do my best to give it to them, as much as I can. I respect them for their hard work and they respect me for mine and they offer to help with the dishes (naturally I say no) and they leave their beds nicely made in the morning and I put a chocolate on each of their pillows to thank them for it when they come home after skiing.

Now I've sliced the meat and I've opened the foie gras tin and I'm cutting it into slender batons. One stick lies in the middle of each slice like a corpse on a rug. I wrap the meat round the foie gras and fold it over, top, and bottom, to make a parcel. I stab two cocktail sticks in to hold it all together, and then on to the next one.

Once they're all rolled up I'll have to sear them in a red-hot frying pan so that they don't lose all their juices and dry out in the oven. I hate that bit. Kitchen full of smoke and droplets of hot fat flying everywhere.

Carlos says that when he fries steak he does it topless because it saves having to wash his clothes. I'd like to be able to watch that one day. No lustful intent, this is Carlos. Carlos is a dear. He wears his wedding ring proudly and he sends all his money home to his wife – their first baby's due in June. He has three jobs here that I know of and whenever anything heavy or dirty needs doing, somehow Carlos is always around to help. He's not angling for tips or anything, he really genuinely enjoys helping people. Just like me. Even that dreadful Mrs Ashbrook-Pembleton-French had to admit it, when he carried her and William's skis all the way up from the lift station because she was too cheap to take a taxi. 'Carlos is *so* obliging.'

Venetia says he has a lunar face – it's just like the moon, round and full of craters – but I don't care. I get him in to sharpen all the knives once a week. I could do it quite well myself really, but it gets him in from the cold and I give him some of yesterday's cake with some special liqueur cream added on top, and we have a good gossip. He even gave me a recipe for feijoada once. It's a spicy bean stew with bits of smoky pork in it – a kind of choucroûte but with beans instead of cabbage. It sounded warming and filling. I tried doing it but I must have done it wrong because everyone got wind the next day, a foggy day it was too, and no skiing. Jerusalem artichokes can be inflationary as well, but of course this time it won't matter.

Every time, I wish they didn't have to go back. When they come home drop-dead tired after skiing and the melting snow plops into their mugs as they drowse over their tea, I look at their happy shining faces and think that this is how they ought to be. Then over dinner some idiot says something about home or the news and you can hear the greyness come into their voices. Wet streets and long commutes and long meaningless hours stuck in offices with bullies for bosses and morons for workmates. Pointless work that *just anybody* could do, if it needed doing at all in the first place. The white snow and blue skies and black runs and red runs and blue runs and green ones all fade into grey and grey and grey and grey and grey. I can see them crumple as they talk. I feel I'm watching a butterfly shrivel up and fade and squeeze back into its chrysalis.

'An experience they will remember for the rest of their lives.' That's our mission statement. Except that three days after they've gone home it'll be as if they've never been here. They'll be exactly the same people they were before they came. As if they'd never lived at all.

This time I'm not going to let it happen.

The next two days' skiing wouldn't have been much anyway. The clouds have come in after a week of sunshine and tomorrow it'll be totally clampers. Nothing will move. They'll sit indoors and snipe at each other and get grumpy and read day-old newspapers and quarrel over what music to put on the state-of-the-art twin sound systems. Today was the best day. Today is the sort of day they should remember till they die.

Now I've scalded the peaches and skinned them and cut out the stones with a small sharp knife. Into the hole goes my own special bitter chocolate mixture. It's the contrast in flavours that makes it a masterpiece.

Carlos brought me the powder. He says it'll dissolve quite easily in the chocolate and the extra bitterness won't be noticed. But I've added a bit of icing sugar as well, just in case. He says I mustn't taste the mixture once I've made it and I must be sure to wash my hands thoroughly after I've done it, even under my nails. It's lucky one of his jobs is cleaning at the pharmacy. Carlos is so obliging.

Tomorrow I'll have some extra tidying up to do, but there won't be any skiing so I won't miss anything. More tidying than usual, but a lot more time to do it in before the new people arrive on Saturday. They'll get bone-dry sheets and pillowcases, all perfectly ironed, no hurry, and the whole chalet will get a really good clean: no need to cut corners for once. If it all goes according to plan, perhaps this time next week I'll try roasting a goose.

Carlos had me worried for a bit. We were laughing over my plan the other day – I think it was before he realised how serious I was – and then he stopped and said, 'If they haven't *left*, where will you *leave* them?' He's proud of his English, and quite right too, it's better than mine.

He had a point. Somehow I hadn't thought of that. I wouldn't want the new guests to feel crowded or jostled or anything. It was a real problem.

I worried over it for a whole day, and then of all people it was that evil Mrs Ashbrook-Pembleton-French who gave me the answer. It was the day before yesterday. Carlos had delivered some heavy supplies and we were in the basement, sorting it out. Cheap wine, bogwash, things like that. It's a big big space carved deep into the rock, so it never freezes in winter and it stays cool and dry all summer, and then I remembered that evil woman and what she'd written in my visitors' book. It was wise advice:

'Cold preserves.'

Not This Time

The carriage was half empty and very dimly lit. No-one else had noticed it in the rush to get on the train. As he sagged into a corner by the door Sen felt a sense of calm triumph, of a risk well taken. It had been Sen who'd said they should try for the train instead of skiing down through the muddy porridge of the lower slopes. It had been Sen who'd led the mad charge at insane speeds down the woodland tracks. It had been Sen, 'dopey Sen,' who'd spotted the short cut that got them to the back of the crowd on the station platform seconds before the gates were locked and the train arrived. And finally it had been Sen and Sen alone who had risked public humiliation by trying the door of the darkened carriage that everyone had been ignoring. Sen, and Sen alone. Terry was on the train, he was sure of it – Swiss mountain trains don't leave people behind – but Terry was in one of the steam-filled people-filled carriages crushed into close encounters with a crowd of overheated one-white-shirt-a-week sweaty lads.

Sen would hear all about it from Terry afterwards, but he didn't mind. Love was good, but coming out on top some-times was nice as well.

Sen wedged himself between the doorway and the glass partition at the end of the nearest row of seats, and sagged carefully until he was perfectly wedged, with every muscle relaxed. He'd had a dog once that used to try to sleep standing up so as to catch the last rays of the afternoon sun. The dog had always failed and gone crashing to the ground, but Sen had worked out how to do the trick. Not only was it very comfortable but it also looked really cool.

Safely cocooned in his inertia, Sen gazed lazily round. Nobody had got on with him and the people in the carriage must have come from higher up. Either they'd got tired early or they were the rucksacked avalanche-transceiver types who consider the lower slopes beneath them. In one direction his view was blocked by the broad shoulders of an unpleasantly large man. For Sen, anyone taller was unpleasantly large, particularly if they stood too close.

In the seat opposite Sen was a very small, very old, very upright Swiss woman. Her face was unreadable. She could be going home to bake cakes or wring the necks of chickens, and whichever it was, she would do it with the same detached and unsentimental expression.

Next to her, two adolescents dozed, their heads close together because they were sharing the same headphones, and beyond them a very small girl in furs was sitting on her father's lap as if it was a throne and she was a queen requiring homage from every person on the train. On Sen's own side of the train, just the other side of the glass panel from him, a rather pretty girl was staring intensely into a mirror and

111

applying lipstick of exactly the same colour as her violently pink headband.

Across the way stood a couple. The man was tall and solid and his face was that oily stubbly reddish brown that you get from a long day's skiing and frequent applications of suntan lotion. Sen loved that texture and would often spend several minutes in the bathroom rubbing his own chin hard against his palm before regretfully shaving it all off and getting ready for dinner. The woman had her back to him; but he could see from the man's eyes that she was beautiful. It was there in the way he looked at her and it was there even more when one of them whispered something into the other's ear, and the eyes and the black brows dissolved into a smile that, even at a distance of eight feet and out of the direct line of fire, made Sen feel he was drowning.

The eyes were what had first drawn him to Terry. A mouth that smiled easily and often, with eyes that never did; and just below the eyes, a look of defiant vulnerability. It had taken Sen weeks to unlock that face and now he was beginning to wonder if he had ever really succeeded at all. Strange, he thought, how you could love someone so badly that just thinking of him made you feel dizzy, and yet at the same time feel such enormous frustration.

Take their arrival here, for instance. Terry had grumbled all through the journey – no, not grumbled, *whinged,* which was worse – about how they were sure to be given the worst room and perhaps even separate beds. And then when they'd turned out to have the best and largest room with the best and largest bed ('because you're the first and anyway you're

112

bound to be the biggest') he'd switched effortlessly to grumbling about condescension instead of prejudice.

Yes, Terry was a couple of years older than Sen. Yes, Terry had a mind-numbingly stressful job and Sen didn't. Yes, Terry would regularly come home on autopilot, sterile cynical zombie mode that lasted long past bedtime. But that was back home, they were here now, they were on holiday. It was a time for relaxation and healing, so when was he going to start?

Sterile cynicism wasn't part of the real Terry, the Terry who reached out in the night. It was just an icy crust that was shutting him in, and Sen had to melt through that ice and reach the warm heart underneath. He could feel it beating sometimes, so close, so close... and then something would happen and he was far away from it again. It was as if the ice was working inwards and the faster he tried to melt through it, the deeper the ice would penetrate. It seemed like a race to see who would get there first, to free Terry's heart or to freeze it. Sen wasn't sure yet whether he'd win.

Superstitiously, Sen turned to the glass of the door and breathed on it.

In Rome, among the quiet expensive villas of the Aventine Hill where few tourists go, there is a wide terrace high above the Tiber. It has a broad balustrade round it, and it's the place where Rome's lovers make their mark. Sometimes there are simple initials or a heart, sometimes there is a name, and once or twice you will see a long, sad letter in desperate felt-tip soaked into the stone, addressed to someone who will never read it and probably doesn't even know it exists. On one of the pillars of that balustrade, eight months before, Sen had taken a key and scratched their first monogram, a T with an S twining round its stem like a snake.

The T.S. had appeared in many places since then: in jam on the surface of porridge; in cream poured onto a bowl of coffee (not very successful); in the dirt on the back of a coach; and even, a couple of nights ago, in unsteady yellow lines in the snow, with neither of them able to remember afterwards who had drunkenly written the T and who had done the S.

It hadn't been Terry's idea in the first place but he'd been strangely understanding about it, even reassuring: 'Just because it's disappeared,' he'd said when Sen was upset by a short-lived T.S., 'it doesn't mean it's gone.'

So now Sen turned to the glass of the door and breathed on it. He drew a T and then he drew an S on top. It wasn't very elegant, the S didn't twine or anything, it just sat; but it would do.

The old woman opposite was staring at him as if he'd committed a major crime. Well, let her. Probably it was. Most things were. But the evidence would have disappeared by the time they got to the next station. In fact it was already fading: the misty circle was getting smaller and smaller and the blank glass was eating into the top bar of the T.

Now that he'd twisted round to make his mark, Sen could see a little past the large man. A vertical pole stood between the two rows of seats and holding on to it was a young, scantily bearded snowboarder. His skinny arms were wound round the pole as if without them he'd collapse into a pool on the floor. His legs were half bent and they really weren't holding him up at all. His belly sagged, his whole body sagged. His head was turned away, but Sen had the feeling that the snowboarder had been looking at him until a moment ago.

If two male animals look each other in the eye then there is trouble. This applies to wolves and dogs and it applies to men as well. Once the eyes are locked the only way out of a fight is for someone to look away, and that someone is the loser. And no-one wants to be a loser.

Avoiding someone else's gaze also marks you down as a loser, so animals have evolved ways of looking away while making sure that honour is preserved. Cats wash; seagulls furiously tear up tufts of grass; executives check their messages – and skiers polish their sunglasses.

The snowboarder might look round at any moment. Sen became aware that his sunglasses were covered in greasy smudges, so he took out his handkerchief and started to polish them. He breathed on each lens in turn, rubbed it, and held it up to the light. If he found that a spot or a streak was left, he did it all again, until finally both lenses were spotless and gleaming. Satisfied, he put the glasses back in his pocket and looked up – and found that everyone was staring at him.

The old woman in black had gone deathly pale and was crossing herself as if she'd seen a ghost. The dark-haired man's girlfriend had turned to look at Sen with a frozen expression on her face, while the man himself clutched her to him with fierce protectiveness. The little queen had wriggled round on her royal throne and was hiding her head in her father's jacket. Even the music-doped adolescents were struggling towards some sort of awareness that the world existed.

Sen looked down to his side, and the lipstick girl on the other side of the glass panel looked up at him, quite white except for the shocking pink lipstick and two red spots glowing on her cheeks. She took out her mirror and breathed heavily on it. She turned it towards Sen with a nervous, propitiatory smile. Sen saw his own face reflected in the mirror, reflected clear and sharp without a trace of mist.

When something really terrible happens the mind goes limp, just as the body goes limp during a really bad skiing fall, until all the bumping and tumbling has stopped and it's possible to work out what's what. Sen had time to put together the clues he'd already seen – the shiny mirror, the darkened carriage, the clean fresh air, everyone's shock when he breathed – but he had no idea what they could add up to. He stood still, his mind detached, all thought suppressed. His face went cold and then hot, and a tingling sensation started in the front of his thighs and spread up the sides of his rib cage.

The pink lipstick girl was tapping on the window to attract his attention. She was trying to explain something else.

'Not now.' It was the big broad-shouldered man who had spoken. He had a deep resonant voice. He'd spoken quietly, but with great authority.

The fact that such a quiet voice was audible made Sen realise that the train had stopped. It had to be a signal or something, because there were no lights visible outside.

Trying to see if there was still light coming from the steam-filled carriage in front, Sen found himself looking straight into the snowboarder's eyes. Their message was not what he had expected.

Yes, you are allowed to look as long as you like, they said.

No, it doesn't matter.

Nothing matters.

I am here.

That is all.

When eyes meet, there are two ways of not starting a fight without actually looking away. One is to be so utterly self-contained that nothing outside you can affect you. The other is to have been hurt so much that nothing really matters any more. You don't try to defend yourself against further pain because in the end even suffering isn't all that interesting. Pain is just something that happens. *Everything* is just something that happens.

It would have been easy for Sen to end it all by looking away – easy but impossible. In this quiet train where only one person was breathing, there could be nothing easier than to look away, polish your glasses again, and read the emergency exit instructions. A minor slip of attention, that's all it would take, a simple accident quickly forgotten. But Sen couldn't do it. He already knew he was incapable of being angry – it used to drive Terry round the bend when they quarrelled – but now he found he had another disability: he was incapable of being cruel. He kept his eyes gently on the young snowboarder.

117

The boy unwrapped himself from the pole and with an effort pulled himself up and stood straight. He took one awkward step forward on those thin legs and then one more, holding tightly on to the overhead straps each time as if to compensate for the lurching motion of the train; except that the train was still immobile.

Sen simply observed. One part of his mind kept him calm by saying that he could end this at any moment: look away for an instant and everything will be normal again. But another part of him was silently dismantling every defence, preparing to be unprotected and to accept whatever was about to happen.

Then a lot did happen, very quickly. Somewhere a signal clanged. The train jerked and shuddered and began to lurch into motion. The carriage lights came fully on and Sen could see the snowboarder's face clearly at last. His soul crumbled into dust. The boy was young indeed – he must be younger than Sen – but his eyes were the eyes of someone who has seen terrible things. No-one that young should have seen that much: no-one of *any* age should be allowed to see that much. His vision blurred with tears, Sen tried to step forward; but the broad-shouldered man's voice spoke out again, loudly over the growing clatter of the train. 'Not this time,' it said. The man turned and thrust Sen aside. Sen heard the smashing of glass, the clank of the emergency lever, the limp sound of the doors flopping open – then the man had seized his arm in a crushing, icy grip and hurled him from the carriage.

Sen landed awkwardly, one knee smashing hard onto unseen stones. He heard his skis land clattering beside him, and the sound of greased cogs meshing together as the train accelerated smoothly away.

Sen dragged himself to a crouching position by the side of the track. He watched the lights of the train disappear round a bend. He was all right. Nothing seemed to be broken, nothing was wrong – only an upper sleeve shredded to powder by the man's cold grip, and the white bruise of frostbite beneath, and the pain just beginning.

Dougie Lewis

Was Dougie Lewis's death an accident? I can never quite remember. If it wasn't, he's had his revenge.

Dougie didn't look the kind of person you could hate that much. He looked like any other overgrown Australian youth doing Europe on a shoestring – except that, unusually, he did have money, enough to pay the rent I was asking for the spare bed in my flat, which in turn meant that I could afford a lift pass. It seemed like the ideal solution – at the time.

Sharing the flat was OK in itself, I suppose. At least, it was no worse than it usually is when two men live together in a cramped studio flat in a skiing resort. Even Dougie's habit of sleeping with the window shut and giving the place an atmosphere could be dealt with by staying awake till I heard the first snore, and then opening the window very quietly. Besides, the morning always comes in the end, and with it sunshine, clean air, and freedom. But that was when the real problem began.

'Just because I sleep with you tonight, it doesn't mean I'll ski with you in the morning.' Either Dougie hadn't read St Anton's most popular T-shirt, or he didn't think it applied to him. Perhaps things are different where he comes from, deep in the Outback. Perhaps men need to stick closer together in Miller's Bottom or whatever he said it was called, with its scrub, its 20,000 sheep, and its two trains a week. Perhaps all the excitement of Thursday's westbound departure can unhinge a man, so that he wanders off and loses himself until he's in danger of missing the further thrill of Tuesday's eastbound arrival – unless his mates stick close to him to keep him from harm. But St Anton isn't Fleapit Hollow (or whatever). It has dozens of trains a day, *and* cable cars *and* chair-lifts. And I certainly didn't need a keeper.

There was no way to tell Dougie this. I tried subtle hints. I tried unsubtle hints, but Dougie was impervious. He didn't even have the decency to be embarrassed about following me around. He just came along.

I tried ignoring him, but he didn't notice. I tried going down things that were too difficult for him – there were plenty of them – but he was too dim to know fear. He'd hesitate at the top and then overtake me half-way down. Sometimes he was with his skis, sometimes he wasn't, but either way, when I got to the bottom there he'd be, standing there brushing the snow out of his hair, grinning crookedly and saying 'rllykll.' I'm not sure if that's how they really say 'really cool' back in Ocker's Arse, or if he got it off the television – do they have TV out there? Anyway that's how he said it, 'rllykll,' as if he'd swallowed his tongue.

One afternoon I took him up onto the ridge west of Kapall – that is, I went up and of course Dougie came along. That was rllykll too. We did the ten-minute climb from the restaurant, and the hairy traverse that gives you time to get seriously scared, and then I pointed my skis straight down and did a whole series of sexy, sinuous curves down the virgin snow. No-one in St Anton can beat my technique, not even Sepp at the ski shop, and anyone who wanted could stand on far-off Galzig and look across at what I'd done, and despair. And then Dougie had joined me, in one piece and as happy as a spaniel. I was glad he'd survived. At least, I was glad *then*. When we got further away and I could see what he'd done to my mountain, I was a lot less glad. My wonderful waves were there – I'd never done them better. Next to them was a crude zigzag that looked as if someone had been laying a chain of matches. The short straight bits were when Dougie was descending out of control, and the big blobs at each corner were where he'd fallen over, to stop himself, and got up facing in the opposite direction.

My favourite fantasy about meeting the girl of my dreams is the one where she's next to me in the cable-car and I touch her shoulder and point to my mountain and say 'I did that' and of course she sort of merges into my arms. Except that now she wouldn't. Now she'd see my lovely lines and Dougie's utter chaos and she'd ask, 'Oh, which one is yours?'

Slowly, I began to hate Dougie Lewis.

I'm not a very efficient hater. I suppose I could have pushed him down a cliff or welded his bindings shut or some-thing, but I didn't even try taking him down somewhere he'd be sure to fall and break his neck. Knowing Dougie's luck, *he'd* have ended up visiting *me* in hospital, and knowing the relaxed chumminess of the folks back in Dingo's Dong, he'd have come to see me every day. Twice a day, even. So I skied cautiously, and I thought hard.

The first thing was to get sane, and the only way to get sane was to get away from Dougie for a while. So I crippled my credit card and booked a day's outing with a mountain guide. The night before, I went to bed early while Dougie went to a nightclub with some people he'd met. I lay there and relaxed and thought about Dougie. He was bound to come home very late and very drunk, but of course he wouldn't let that stop him skiing hard tomorrow. Which in turn meant that in the afternoon he'd probably fall asleep. What made this such a desirable fantasy was that Dougie had recently taken to sunbathing on the railway line after skiing – cheapest sundeck in the resort, rllykll. He had a running battle with the police about it, and I'd warned him that the main Zurich-to-Vienna railway line was rather busier than the one at Gruesome Gulch, but he said not to worry, he knew the timetable. So tomorrow he'd be sunbathing on the tracks, and he'd fall asleep, and the train would come, and I wouldn't have anything to worry about any more.

The crash woke me. Dougie had fallen over his bedside cupboard. It was 2 a.m.

But somehow, when Dougie's alarm clock woke us at seven the next morning, *I* was the one with the hangover, and *he* bounced out of bed and into the shower before I could bring myself to move. Eventually I dragged myself to the ski school meeting-place and set off on my expedition.

Dougie looked as if he was going to come along even though he wasn't invited, but he realised just in time that it would cost him more money than he had. I was free.

The guide took me up to the top of the Valluga and we skied down the back. The landscape was unlike anything I'd come across before. There were huge powder bowls that you had to walk up out of at the end, and precipitous descents where falling was, as my guide carefully put it, 'inadvisable.' There was powder and windslab and crust and spring snow and finally a vast flat expanse of crème brûlée straight out of Scott of the Antarctic. Finally we found ourselves in Zürs, of all places, and squeezed into the bus back to St Anton.

I felt glad to be alive, which was something I hadn't felt for a while, and I was even quite happy when I ran into Dougie at the pizzeria across the road. We played it by the rules. I told him all about my day, while he half listened, and then he told me all about his day, while I half listened. Fair's fair. He didn't seem to have minded being left on his own, but then Dougie never minded anything much. In any case, he must have found someone to ski with, because 'we' had spent all day going up the Schindler chairlift and down the red and black runs under it (I wondered what 'we' thought of Dougie's head-first skiing methods) and 'we' had found all the remaining tiny patches of untracked snow and carved them to pieces. All but one, said Dougie. There was one untouched hump that was visible from the chairlift. It fascinated him.

'It'd be really cool to ski that,' he told me.

'Well, if it's been untouched for so long, it's got to be totally inaccessible.' I yawned. Dougie's impractical enthusiasm was starting to irritate me again.

'Couldn't we climb up it?'

'It's too steep on one side, and there's a sheer drop on the other.' I couldn't be sure; but then neither could he.

Dougie thought for a bit. 'There's always above,' he said. I was busy eating, so he went on. 'I heard about this place in Val d'Isère. There's this chairlift that goes over a ridge from one bowl to the next, and on top of the ridge there's a place you can see ski tracks, where people have jumped off in the middle. I'm sure you can do that here. It's just no-one's thought of it.'

I should have stopped him then. I should have told him not to be such a moron. I should have told him to stick to the nursery slopes, where he belonged – but I didn't. I said nothing. Now, that could have been malice or it could have been simple tiredness. I can't remember the truth of it any more. Perhaps I even spent the meal pleading with him not to take such a suicidal risk. Or I may have spent it watering the idea and making it grow. I just don't know.

We were almost the first ones up the mountain. One good thing about Dougie, he did get up early. We took the first stage of the Valluga lift up to Galzig, great when there are no queues, and then some pretty flat runs with a T-bar in the middle took us over to Schindler. The sky was clear as usual, and the snow was all frozen porridge, with ruts – that's the trouble with spring – but a thin veil of cloud on the horizon suggested that a major dump was on its way. Dougie picked up a lump of ice and took it up the chairlift with him. He counted the pylons aloud – one, two, three, four, five – and ahead of us, on the side of the ridge, I could see a small patch of untouched snow, just as Dougie had said. The chair swung down from the fifth pylon and he switched to counting seconds as the ground rushed up towards us – one, two, three, four, ... and on 'eleven' he let go of his lump of ice, and twisted round to see exactly where it would land, some twenty feet below us. 'Bullseye,' Dougie shouted. I gripped tightly onto the safety bar as we swung out over the next chasm.

Dougie's excitement took him down the run past the Ulmerhütte with un-Dougie-like competence, and we got to the bottom of the chairlift in one piece despite the icy conditions. I'd like to remember that I begged him not to do it, but I can't. I must have, though. I must have offered him distractions and alternatives – the back side of the Kandahar, dodging in and out of the trees – off-piste Osthang with its electricity pylons and its waist-high moguls. Surely I did? I'll never know, now; but if I did, it didn't work. We went up anyway.

One pylon, two, three, four – I opened the safety bar for him – five. One second, two seconds, ... eight seconds, nine, ten, eleven. Dougie slid out. The chair lurched and I held on tight to stop myself falling out, and I listened for the sound of his landing.

A wet, crunchy, cracking sound. You know, when you're pulling a chicken to pieces and a bone comes out of its socket? The same sound exactly. The landing site was hidden behind the ridge but there wouldn't have been any point in looking anyway, not after that.

Any noise out of him, and I could have believed he was still alive, but there was nothing. When a scream did come, it was too high-pitched to be Dougie, and too close as well. It went on and on. Someone on the chair behind must have seen what had happened. I could see it too. A brightly coloured mass in an impossible position, and blood seeping into the white snow. It was too far away and behind a ridge, but every time I shut my eyes, it was there. It still is.

I heard afterwards that his ski had broken and slashed open an artery.

The clatter of the next pylon drowned the screaming. The lift took five minutes to get me to the top, five minutes for Dougie Lewis to lie bleeding to death in a snowdrift. Not that he needed that long. All the way up, I held on to the safety bar and kept my eyes shut, watching Dougie's blood. I was still holding on when the chair got to the top. I was still holding on when it swung round its pillar on the start of its journey down, so the automatic brake tripped and the lift stopped and they wound it back a bit and I staggered off and slumped in an out-of-the-way corner while the radios shouted and the lift re-started. The next people to arrive were the ones who'd actually seen it happen. They were a bit better than me, because they got off the lift all right, but they didn't manage to do much else, they just skied helplessly into the nearest bit of safety net. It's nice to know those nets work. At last someone calmer arrived, and what he said made them stop the lift at once. Long radio conversations. The lift started again and ran until everyone who had been on it was safely off. It stopped. More radio. It started again, slowly. The rescuers, someone said.

But I knew there was nothing to rescue.

Much later, they got me onto the chair with someone responsible next to me. He closed the safety bar and held it closed. He didn't need to. The lift started, going backwards this time. I tried to enjoy the novel experience of going down a chairlift.

I counted five pylons and then realised it didn't help, I had no idea how many pylons you had to count if you were going down. So I stopped, and shut my eyes, and watched Dougie bleed again.

At the bottom of the chair there was a piste-basher, and they put me on it and drove me in style all the way down the Steissbachtal and into St Anton. How Dougie would have loved it all, riding home in triumph. I wondered if they'd taken him down the same way.

I expected the police would be asking me what had happened, and I tried to work out what to say. But the police weren't much interested. They'd never liked Dougie much. Once they'd established that he'd jumped and not fallen, and that there was no danger of claims for compensation, they didn't care about anything else. They sent someone back to the flat to get Dougie's passport and look for anything that had his home address on it, and that was that. They left me alone.

All the next day, I stayed indoors. The promised front had arrived and it was chucking it down. The town was silent except for the muffled thumps of distant artillery trying to set off avalanches. Some time during the day they came and packed up all of Dougie's things. I went out drinking that evening but I came home early. Going out isn't the same when you have no-one to avoid.

I opened the window wide before going to bed, because I had no-one to stop me. All night I was too cold to sleep but too sleepy to shut the window. When I did doze off, I was back on the chairlift again.

Dougie's alarm woke me up at seven the next morning. They must have forgotten to take it. I lay there and counted thirty of its thirty-two beeps, aiming to leap out of bed at the last possible moment and make it to the bathroom before Dougie did. I won, of course. I always would win, now.

The cold front had passed. The sky was a rich blue, and the tops of the mountains shone white in the sunlight. Even the village streets were covered in snow. It was the kind of day that skiers dream of. It was my duty to make something of it.

I was just pulling on my ski boots when I heard the voices. Some guys with snowboards were passing by on their way to the lift, and they stopped for a moment outside my window. There was a gap in the conversation and I heard someone say 'really cool.' It was nothing like the way Dougie used to say it, but it was enough. I gave up the effort. I took off the boot, and put on my trainers. I wasn't ready, yet, to face a world full of Dougie's accent, Dougie's catchphrases, anoraks like Dougie's, and the colour red against the white snow. Even being dead didn't seem to stop him following me around. I needed to escape.

I went to the station and waited for the next train to Innsbruck. It was hot in the sun, but there were no sunbathers on the tracks, and on the platform there were just two old women in furs, and a large crate.

The train to Zurich airport came first, and the crate was lifted aboard. I read the label. 'LEWIS,' it said, 'Miller's Hollow, WA, Australia. ZRH–BKK–PER.' He had followed me here as well.

The Innsbruck train came next, and I got on it. I counted the pylons as they went past. Then I counted the thumps that the wheels made on the track: one, two, three, four, five, six, seven, eight, nine, ten – but when 'eleven' came it was always in Dougie's voice. So I stopped myself counting and looked at the piles of limestone ballast by the side of the track. Back home in Australia they probably use sand instead of limestone. That made me think of the sand they sprinkle on the pavements in cities when somebody's jumped out of a window and they've finished tidying up the mess. I wondered what they'd used on Dougie's red-and-white snow.

Innsbruck is an odd sort of a place. It's a mile up in the air but it looks like any ordinary provincial town. It gets very hot indeed, even in March. The park had tropical-looking flowers, and little flocks of green parakeets were flying from tree to tree, which looked surreal against the background of white mountain peaks. I did the sights in an hour and a half

– town hall, Golden House, and all – and then I wandered through grey, dusty streets until I ended up in a café by the main road, where two or three dumpling-faced Austrians were playing video games. In the end I couldn't stand it any more and I went back to the station. The bookstall was selling the same blockbuster spy book that Dougie had been reading, three pages a night, the one I'd nearly finished when he wasn't looking. I didn't buy it. I just took the train home.

I sat in one corner of the compartment, by the window. It was the only seat that didn't face a photograph of snowy mountains. Just before the train left, a small dark-haired girl came in and took the seat furthest from me, by the door. The train started moving, and as I tried not to count pylons again, the door slid open and a party of Americans looked in, large Americans in thick sweaters. Four of them came in and sat down, filling the compartment: the rest went further down the train somewhere. I buried myself behind an Austrian Railways brochure and tried to look European and unapproachable. To my amusement, the girl did the same.

The Americans threw their bags on the rack, took out their chewing-gum, and settled down to a detailed discussion of the game of ice-hockey they'd just won. They also took off their shoes. Eventually they settled down to sleep. But their socks didn't. I calculated how far we had to go before St Anton. It was impractical to try to hold my breath till then.

For a few minutes, all was silence. Then I saw the girl in the corner put down her brochure and lie down on the floor. She stretched her arm out towards me. I was puzzled to know how to respond, but then she reached out and took the discarded left shoe of the American opposite me and stealthily drew it towards herself. She did the same with his neighbour's left shoe; then she stood up, bent down, and picked up the left shoes of the two sleepers nearest her. She slid the door open slowly, so that there wouldn't be a sudden change in the noise to disturb them, and disappeared, carrying the shoes. A little later, she reappeared, without the shoes. She slowly slid the door shut again, and sank back into reading about the corporate history of the Austrian railway system. She didn't look at me.

When the train stopped at St Anton, the hockey players barely stirred. I stepped carefully over their legs and got out. They didn't move. The girl was there on the platform. I waited till the train was moving away before I spoke.

'Where did you put them?' I asked.

'Out of the window.'

'Why just the left shoes?'

'Less to carry. And you can't make a pair out of two right ones. The SAS did it during the war. Not trainers, but aircraft wings. It saved explosives.'

I was enchanted by her knowledge of military history and its applications. 'So how did you know they were going further than us?'

'Oh, I didn't,' she said lightly. 'Coffee?'

Why not, I thought. It's not as if I've got anything to go home to. We settled down in the station buffet, and I studied her upturned nose.

'What did you think I was doing?' she asked.

'I honestly had no idea. I knew you weren't doing it because you liked shoes.'

'Why?'

'You'd have taken both. And it wasn't *me* you were after. I mean, women lying on the floor with their arms outstretched, all right, I'm used to that, but in *public...*'

She had grey eyes. They were perfectly inexpressive. She could see right through me but I still couldn't see an inch into her. She might as well have been wearing mirrored sunglasses.

'What do you like having for breakfast?' she asked.

There is an age at which boys think this is a sophisticated and subtle chat-up line. I'd long since grown out of it (Dougie hadn't, quite), but in any case I'd never heard a woman use it.

The grey eyes were looking at my right ear now, or even just past it. 'Waffles,' she said. 'Waffles and baked beans. Waffles and eggs. Waffles and eggs and beans. Waffles and maple syrup. Canadian bacon and maple syrup.'

I looked behind me. There was a menu painted up on the wall, white letters on a black board. High-calorie food for skiers. Everything short of deep-fried Mars bars.

I turned back to her and said 'Stir-fried waffles in black bean sauce,' and there was amusement in the corners of those eyes, I was sure of it.

'7.15,' she said. It wasn't a question.

'7.30.' I had to assert myself somehow. I felt entirely out of my depth. Actually, that wasn't a bad feeling at all.

Thanks to Dougie's alarm clock I was there at 7.25. She wasn't there. I had no idea how much of a joke yesterday had been, or if it had been only yesterday's joke and not today's. Still, I could cover my uncertainty easily enough. They did breakfasts, so I ordered breakfast. Not waffles, though.

She came in while I was in the middle of a loud bit of toast. She was wearing her ski boots, which made me glad I'd come in mine. There was no discussion but it was obvious we were going to ski together. There was something in her eyes again, and again I didn't know what.

I let her choose where we went. My excuse to myself was that I didn't want to embarrass her by asking her how well she could ski. We went up Galzig, and down, and up the long chairlift. I looked across at the mountainscape to our right, and saw with relief that the snow had obliterated the tracks that Dougie and I had made a few days before. Now I'd have an opportunity to make uncontaminated ones.

Coming off the chairlift, we turned right and then left, and suddenly I couldn't breathe, because that was the way across to the Schindler lift. I tried to catch her up and tell her to stop, but she was faster than me. What could I have said, anyway? I couldn't have explained.

We slid straight onto the first chair (it was too early for queues) and I was whisked into the air on my appointment with Fate.

I turned my head away so that she couldn't see that my eyes were shut, and I counted the pylons by their sound. One, two, three, four... when we got to six I'd be safe. 'Look,' she said excitedly, 'look there!' and she grabbed my arm and pulled me round so that I could see what she'd seen. I couldn't help myself. I looked down at the site of the disaster.

It had been a good dump. A thick, even, untouched blanket of white covered everything, stones, boulders, everything. I couldn't even see any ski tracks, just the rhythmic swell of the landscape. It was blank, blank, blank.

Except that passing directly below us, coming down from the ridge that Dougie had wanted to ski from, was a single track. It was rather a messy track. A crude zigzag of short straight lines connecting big irregular blobs. It started nowhere in particular and it didn't really go anywhere. In a couple of seconds the ridge blocked the track from our sight, but I recognised the style. It was unique, and its author was at that moment lying in a box at Bangkok airport, waiting for his flight to Perth.

'Just because I ski with you today, it doesn't mean I'll sleep with you in the night.' Well, perhaps it will, perhaps it won't. I don't mind. She has a sense of humour, that's good, and if she's laughing at me – well, that's better than pity. And I know already what she likes for breakfast.

It's nice to have someone to ski with. I hope I'm not following her when I shouldn't, like Dougie.

Wherever we go, I see more of those zigzag tracks. They're always on blank inaccessible patches of snow, and they're always connected by these big shapeless blobs.

OK, Dougie, I'll let you go now. I'll rent the space to someone else and he'll snore in bed and he'll fart and argue about the window and do all the things you did and it won't be the same, it won't be the same and I'll still miss you, Dougie. I'll miss you always. But when I get up early on a sunny morning after snow and I look at the impossible places that no-one can get to, I'll see your mark. Line, blob, line. Line, shapeless blob, line.

Never stop, Dougie Lewis. Don't ever stop.

Dorian Gray

Really, the whole thing was all his fault.

I was finishing lunch when I spotted him. He was standing at the bar, chatting to Gemma. Gemma's my dearest friend. She's elegantly slender – though some people might call it scrawny – and she's got long blonde hair... but you know how quickly blondes age. Perhaps that's the reason she's a quick mover, to make up for the lack of time, but really she seems to attract the most unsuitable people. Like that sweet Colombian boy who turned out to have a tattoo. I'm sure it's because she has no mother out here with her to give her advice. Thank goodness she's got me. I'm her friend.

He had nice square shoulders and a suntan that wasn't the usual horrible orange you get in the mountains. Very straight black hair that came down in a fringe and made you want to riffle your fingers through it. Good thick eyebrows that thought of meeting in the middle but decided not to – never trust a man whose eyebrows meet. A permanent cheerful grin – but that could easily have been Gemma, she has that effect... on the undiscerning at least. A one-piece ski suit in black and white and yellow and pink that had come to him through some 1980s time warp. Perhaps it was his father's.

Definitely enough to bowl an impressionable girl over. I mean, he nearly impressed even me. It looked as if poor Gemma needed a friend to rescue her. I was her friend, so she needed *me*.

Gemma skips meals. That's always a mistake. I *never* neglect my food. Real men appreciate women who eat, just as they appreciate real curves. I finished the last remnant of my goulash soup – nothing else is edible in mountain restaurants – and went across to them. Gemma let out a joyful cry and gave me a hug. 'Juliet, how lovely, this is my new friend Harry, I met him on the chairlift.' (So I was right). 'Harry, this is Juliet, she's my best friend.' Then, to help us share fully in her joy, she made sure that her new friend and her *best* friend were as far as possible from each other.

Gemma is not sensible. She should have put me in the middle, between them. As it was, with me on one side of her and Harry on the opposite side, she couldn't face one of us without turning her back to the other. A lady never turns her back on anyone. So she sort of oscillated, poor thing, facing half one way, half the other way, while I had a good chance to observe Harry over her shoulder and he could observe me too. Only if he happened to want to, of course.

He didn't look any worse close up. The eyebrows really did grow like that naturally, he hadn't had to shave the middle bit. And that enchanting notch on the left one wasn't a piercing after all. That was good: piercings and tattoos are the same thing really. If you look closely, most boys have notched eyebrows, it comes from having fights with your friends when you're eight and hitting your head on things.

Girls get scars from their friends too, but our scars are deep inside – and that's where we keep them.

I'm not a snob like my mother – imagine, on the first day she goes round the ski lifts *tipping the lift operators* – but it was reassuring to discover that, as Mother would put it, he 'spoke English.' All in all, he was too good for Gemma, really. She wouldn't be able to appreciate him. What a pity she'd...

I caught sight of the clock and pulled at Gemma's arm with a startled little cry.

'Gemma! Look at the time!'

'Ten past two. Yes?'

'Gemma, your lesson with Jean-Loup, it's at half past!' Jean-Loup was her private ski instructor. Five foot two of gnarled twisted Swiss pine. He was two hundred years old at least and you could follow him down a foggy piste just by following the scent of tobacco. But he was a phenomenal teacher and – as they say – reassuringly expensive. Gemma's family aren't rich. It was my *duty* to remind her not to waste her money. It was my duty as a friend.

Harry understood perfectly. He escorted Gemma to the door with inexorable kindness, and went outside to help her with her skis and make sure she left. Quite right too. It was no more than one would expect of him.

I watched them both go. I glanced at the clock. A gentleman doesn't leave a lady standing all alone at the bar. If he wasn't a gentleman then he was no loss. If he was one...

I looked at the clock again. I'd give him five minutes.

Harry was back in four. He had understood perfectly.

The sun was blasting down and turning the snow into a squishy mess, so we kept to the exact edge of the shade, with our heads in the warm sun and our feet on nice cold snow. All the long-lunch lunatics went zooming past in the sunshine. A girl in a yellow bikini came down in a snow-plough so wide that, well, you could drive a snowplough through it. I don't want to sound like my mother, but really I don't approve of women behaving as if they're in a porno movie. Start behaving as if you were, Mother says, and that's where you'll end up. Following the bikini girl was a boy in small turquoise Speedos carrying the rest of their stuff. I watched him carefully, because he skied rather well. I glanced across at Harry, who was watching them both with roughly equal interest. He slid across to me. 'I can't help thinking,' he said with a smile, 'what will happen when he catches an edge on the ice.' He scraped the nearest bump with the tip of his ski pole. The snow was as glittery as freshly cut marble. And as rough.

It was our first run, so of course I let him lead. A man is naturally better than a woman at skiing, but this can't happen unless the woman first discovers just how good the man naturally is. In this case, pretty good. I was glad. I'd have had to play dumb otherwise, and playing dumb is such a bore.

The other thing you have to decide with men (Mother says) is whether to be a brainless brunette or well up to his weight intellectually. It's a horrible dilemma. If you get it wrong, you scare them off by admitting that you have a mind, especially if they're English. Or if you get it wrong the other way, you cripple yourself for ever. Imagine going round pretending you're six inches shorter than you really are, when you didn't need to. Playing dumb is *such* a bore. That's not a problem that Gemma has. No man needs to feel threatened when Gemma is around. Gemma is lucky in some ways.

The queue for the chairlift was long and it gave me plenty of time for subtle research. What a relief: he didn't mind me reading books. In fact he'd not only read all the ones I'd read, but others as well. Lucky I'm not Gemma. Any man who reads all the magazines Gemma reads – well, let's just say he's not a man.

It was when we moved on to plays that I began to sense something wrong. I couldn't see how anyone our age could be as erudite as him. He just wouldn't have had the time.

Then he gave himself away completely. I mentioned a play I'd seen over Christmas, and of course he'd seen it too, and he said something about comparing it to the original production. Now English is my forte, I'm not that strong on sums – but even I could work out that the original production had been when I was about minus two years old. I had a good look at Harry. There was no sign of anything that could make him older than 20. *Nothing.* Childishly, I blurted out a simple direct question: 'How old are you?'

It is *not* an illegitimate question. The only people who lie about their age are nobodies who know they'll never make it into Who's Who. Everyone but the nobodies knows that. But it does sound a bit schoolgirlish all the same.

He thought for a moment. I could see the open expression on his face close as if someone had pulled down the shutters over it. Then a little gleam peeped between the slats. 'Oh, older than you think,' he said. 'In fact, much older than you can imagine. You've heard of Dorian Gray, of course?'

Of course I had. Silly question. Dorian Gray was —

But we were at the front of the queue now and the chair-lift slammed us in the calves, the way they do, and we were flying through the air together. Only, a moment before that, an encumbered parent had waved a child at Harry and Harry had nodded and the next thing I knew, there was an infant dumped on the seat between us, and the safety bar was slammed down to keep it in. One of those crash-helmeted fearless four-year-olds that go zipping between your legs just when you're picking your way down something really tricky. You fall and they don't. What with trying to talk French to it and playing games with it to stop it wriggling out, Harry was fully occupied and I had time to think.

The Picture of Dorian Gray (note: Picture, *not* Portrait, everyone gets that wrong) is a longish story by Oscar Wilde and we've been doing it for A level. Like a lot of the Naughty Nineties, it's morbid and soggy, like a huge over-ripe peach. Dorian Gray is an unnecessarily beautiful young man who acquires a lot of vices very quickly and goes round ruining people. All this high living among the low life ought to turn him into a spotty leering flesh-heap but somehow it doesn't. *Because,* early on, an obsessed artist painted him in all his radiant beauty and now all the hangovers and broken veins and blotches and sags happen to the painting and not to him.

I *said* it was all Harry's fault. He shouldn't have put such a far-fetched idea into the head of a pure-minded innocent young girl. The thing was, apart from the minor detail of being impossible, it did explain such a lot about him. Such as his retro 1980s Mondrian ski suit. Such as his familiarity with the acting career of Dame Edith Evans. Such as his general air of maturity. Apart from being impossible it was exactly right. If it was a joke, which of course it was, it wasn't a bad one. Not bad at all.

The end of the lift came. I lifted the bar and we skied away before the departing chair could thump us on the back of our heads. Harry had the child firmly under one arm. Consciously or unconsciously, he was ticking the 'good with children' box with me, big time. The child couldn't decide whether being swooped through the air in the arms of a stranger was exciting or frightening. Then it spotted its father and opted for 'frightening'. It clung to his legs and hid behind them and yelled and yelled. Harry acknowledged the father's embarrassed thanks and we rather hurriedly shuffled away. I heard Harry say, half to himself, 'children, the best contraceptive.' I considered raising a well-bred eyebrow at this, it seemed altogether too far too fast – but I can't, it's my secret tragedy, I can only raise both of them at once and it's not the same thing at all, it means something quite different. So I decided to change the subject instead.

'Where's your picture, then?' I asked.

'Picture?' He sounded puzzled.

'Your portrait. Your ageing portrait. The one with all the spots. Where do you keep it?' I pushed off down the path towards the next lift, leaving him to work it out.

'Not a painting.' He glided up silently beside me. He'd been thinking. 'Paintings are too, too *vieux jeu*. Photograph! Passport photograph!'

He floated off to one side to let some boy racers through.

'And when it expires,' I called across to him, 'do *you?* Expire as well?'

'Not at all. New passport, new photograph. New beginning. It all begins again.' He said it with relish.

He paused. If it was still a joke, I thought, it was starting to wear out. He must have thought so too, because he slid up close to me and took control. 'Round the next corner,' he said, 'wait for my signal, then schuss!'

And that's what happened. We rounded the corner and the path opened out into a broad snowfield that dipped down and then up again to the distant button lift. He signalled, and shot off. I waited a moment and then did the same.

I *hate* schussing. You're crouched up in a ball and you have no control at all. Your skis decide what happens. If they throw you off then you have a long, long walk ahead of you, and even if it goes right, it's all over too quickly. As someone said about something else, "the position is undignified and the pleasure fleeting."

I could see some ridges across the path. I held my breath and clenched everything I could. One, two, three hard bumps kicked up through my boots. They bent my knees further than I thought they would ever go and my teeth felt as if they'd gone up through the back of my head. But I was all there. I'd survived. Still moving fast, I stood up and breathed. At that moment a final ridge that I hadn't seen at all catapulted me far into the sky.

Splat! My skis slapped flat onto the ground. My boots were still attached to my skis. My feet were still in my boots. My body was still on top of my feet – and it stayed there. I'd survived *again*. I shouted out loud and the people waiting for the lift cheered. Harry didn't seem to be among them. I looked round to see where he was. It was only a glance; but my balance went the wrong way, and I went flying.

By the time I'd got my ski on again, Harry was sailing towards me, upright and stately. Was it the light, or had his hair suddenly gone white? Was the magic of the passport wearing off? He came closer, and the whiteness of his shoulders indicated a simpler explanation.

'I see,' he said carefully and maturely, 'that you had the same idea as me. In the end there is only one way to be really sure of the snow conditions – direct empirical verification.' We both laughed and he presented his back to me so that I could dust him off. I reached up to his shoulders and patted him about a bit.

'Juliet.' His voice had an emotional thrill in it that I hadn't heard from him before.

'Juliet, every time you touch me, I can feel a chill run down my spine.' The vibration in his voice came all the way from his diaphragm, and I can tell you, it resonated deep in mine. But there was a suppressed gurgle in it that shouldn't have been there. I didn't trust that gurgle. I was right. He unzipped his ski suit and fished out a large lump of snow from the small of his back. He shook himself thoroughly and his hair became young and black again.

Standing behind him in the lift queue, I could see his bum-bag had come unzipped. Inside, there was something purple with a straight edge. His passport? Well, we could end *that* silly game at least. It was about time.

But Harry had eyes in the back of his head. He spotted my movement before I started it, and did the zip up firmly.

If only he'd been honest with me at that moment. It really *was* all his fault.

Keeping his hand over the bag, he stepped to one side, caught the approaching button, put it between his legs, and went bounding up the slope like a kangaroo. It has to be said that no-one looks dignified being dragged up a hill by the buttocks.

After that, it was, as they say, downhill all the way until, at the bottom of the longest mogul field in creation, we stopped to catch our breath and get our legs back. He'd shrugged out of the top of his ski suit some time before. The suit looked even sillier, if anything, with the sleeves tied round his waist like a giant nappy, but his T-shirt clung to his back. It clung informatively, and that made up for everything.

'Juliet, my dear,' he said in a grown-up voice, 'I am weak at the knees.' But I could hear that gurgle again.

'Your 45-year-old knees?' Silly of me but I couldn't help it.

'90 at least. I should have brought spares. Quick, before they seize up!' He pushed himself over the lip of the final bowl and was gone.

It was one of those end-of-the-day this-is-the-end-of-everything bowls, full of granular brown porridge that had been snow once upon a time, heaped into random piles and punctuated with petrified jelly-kneed beginners and the occasional absurd abandoned toboggan. Through it all, a few complacent souls on freeriders floated down as if this was the most natural medium in the world – which, for them, it was.

At the bottom of it all, a patch of shining slush and a Soviet-style blockhouse that was the bottom station of the cable car. Not a bar in sight to help you down. Only in Austria do they really know how to put bars where they're needed.

I watched him shoot straight down through that horrible gunge. When his speed got too neck-breaking he jumped and kicked violently with both feet at the nearest porridge-heap and scattered it generously over the landscape. Then straight ahead again, faster and faster, until it was time to lose speed again. I'm not at all sure he didn't bury a toddler or two on the way. What had happened to those weak knees of his? Hadn't I tired the man *at all?*

He finished with a controlled glide from snow to slush and from slush to water-skiing, and a sudden lurching halt as his skis stopped dead on the gritty mud beneath. He must have hired them. He stomped sprawlily with one ski onto the back of the other one to release the binding, stepped out with that foot and repeated the movement in reverse. I can tell

you, it is extremely hard to do this move without falling over.
I've watched boys practising it in quiet corners.

It was my turn, and I did what Mother would have done.
I traversed gracefully all the way round the edge of the bowl
to where one of the blue runs came in, dropped steeply into
it and floated down towards him with controlled velocity and
perfect poise. Well before the awkward slush, I stopped,
poked my poles into the latches of my bindings, and leant
back to undo both of them at once. It's not as spectacular as
the sprawly move but it's at least as hard to do without falling
over, and in any case a lady never opens her legs wide in
public even when she is getting out of her skis.

Harry had taken his sunglasses off and he was watching
me. He had very green eyes.

'Will you join us for tea?'

'Us?'

'My father and me.'

'The one you're old enough to be.' That silly game was
addictive.

'No, you've got it the wrong way round. He's not as
young as he's going to be, but he will be soon. We're staying
above the chemists, it's on the way to your hotel.'

'All right, I'd love to.' I didn't have much choice if I
didn't want to be rude.

'You'll enjoy meeting him. He's a great connoisseur.' Of
what, I wondered.

He steered me through the crowded streets with the
lightest of touches on my arm. 'Fingertip control,' my dance

teacher calls it. Boys take time to learn that. Harry was either supremely confident or supremely shy.

We took our boots off outside and padded into the flat in our socks. It was very warm – hot, really – but with a nice smell of polished pine. Harry went off to put the kettle on and I stood around trying to stop my prescription sunglasses misting up. Looking at the chest of drawers where Harry had dumped his stuff, something caught my eye. Something rectangular and purple and gold. His passport must have fallen out.

Now I could end that silly game once and for all and have a properly grown-up tea party with him and his father, impressing them with my cool metropolitan sophistication. I stood very still and listened. Low voices from the kitchen and an occasional clatter. I had time.

I picked up the passport and looked at the final page. RAMSAY, it said, and then, on the next line, HENRY JOHN PERCEVAL. Definitely Harry's, then. I looked down to the date of birth.

My heart missed a beat. And a half.

The impossible had come true, and I was holding it in my hands. That date. That man I'd laughed and chatted and skied with all afternoon. That man was – that man was…

Holding my breath I removed my thumb from the photograph. It was exactly right. It fitted in with what the passport said and with everything that Harry had been trying to tell me. It was Harry all right. Fatter round the chin than I'd seen him, and thinner round the cheekbones. Grey, not white like when he'd fallen in the snow, but vigorous, thick, manly straight grey hair. Quite sexy, really, for a photograph.

At the end of the Oscar Wilde story Dorian Gray eventually has a fit of conscience (unlikely but necessary for the plot) and slashes the evil, leering portrait with a knife. His servants find him dead of stab wounds, wrinkled and horrible, at the foot of a portrait they've never seen, of him in his innocent radiant youth. His corpse is so shrivelled, they only recognise him by the rings he is wearing. I *said* it was an overripe story.

I admit that not all of this tragic tale is Harry's fault. The next bit was the fault of my fingers. I watched them as they tried to tear the page. 'Direct empirical verification,' you see. They struggled with the thick plastic covering. Somehow my teeth came to their aid, and once the tear had started it progressed steadily down the page. I couldn't have stopped it if I'd tried. As it reached the middle of the photograph, I heard a crash from the kitchen and Harry swearing loudly. A moment's pause, and his voice came from the doorway. 'Sorry, slight hitch. We'll be ready in a moment.'

His voice sounded even richer and rumblier than when I'd been brushing the snow off him. I could feel the vibrations. I looked up from the passport. Before I moved my head to look, I knew what I'd see – and I saw it. It was the Harry of the passport. The same bright green eyes, the same tanned skin, but the hair grey, the face thinner, cheerful smile-wrinkles round the eyes. He looked down at my hands and what they held. He looked puzzled. He hadn't grasped yet what had just happened to him. I didn't wait for him to catch sight of himself in a mirror. I dropped the passport, turned, and ran.

No time to put my boots on. I picked them up, and my skis and everything, and ran through the streets in my thick socks, desperate to get back to the hotel, to safety.

I made it. No-one came running after me. I tumbled in through the doors, left my stuff in a heap downstairs, and with the last of my strength staggered into my room and threw myself on the bed.

There was a note from Mother saying she'd gone off to have a drink with a friend and would be back for dinner. I was relieved she wasn't there, asking for explanations.

I lay on my bed and shivered.

I lay *in* my bed and shivered.

I lay in a very hot bath and shivered.

I got together enough strength to send her a message that I wasn't going to be down for dinner. I went to bed but I was too frightened to sleep. Every time I shut my eyes I could see Harry's new face, with its smiling eyes and its deep wrinkles. It looked a kind face, but that didn't mean anything. It was before he'd known what had happened to him.

The trouble when something impossible happens is that you don't know what the rules are. What would Harry do when he noticed the change? What would he do when he realised who had done it? Would he be calm and mellow in his new, kind face, or would he be out for revenge? I could cope with either. It was the not knowing *which* that was so hard.

There was a quiet knock at the door. Startled, I sat up in bed. A moment later the knock came again. Perhaps it was my mother, come to see how I was. I got out of bed and opened the door. It wasn't Mother, it was Harry, still in his ski suit, *young* Harry looking as if nothing had happened. 'Hello Juliet,' he said, 'I just wanted to make sure you were all right. It's all right, really, nothing's happened.' He put his arms round me and kissed me. I can't say if it lived up to expectations because it was the kind of kiss you *live*, you don't pause to evaluate it. I was lost in it. It was a long kiss. Long. Then his lower lip came off in my mouth and started to twitch. I spat it out and looked at his hair coming out in handfuls as I stroked it. Long straight white hair. 'Nothing's happened,' said the fleshless face, skin stretched over bone.

I sat up in bed and screamed. The sheets were wet with my perspiration. Outside, I could hear people shouting and laughing as they went home from the clubs. I got out of bed and went to the bathroom to splash my face with water. I looked up at the mirror, and I was old – old. My face was a mass of fine wrinkles and my fingers were bony and lumpy. I saw someone behind me and I turned. It was Harry, young Harry back again, young Harry laughing and waving the two halves of my passport at me.

I sat up in bed and whimpered. I listened to the quiet outside. I watched the clock move from 5.00 to 5.01. I watched the clock move from 5.01 to 5.02. Perhaps I really was awake this time. I was suddenly very hungry. I went across to the minibar and looked inside. There were no gruesome surprises, no heads of Harry, young or old, but there wasn't anything edible either, only a packet of cashew nuts. I settled down to watch the clock until it was time for breakfast. I tried to pass the time by worrying about how to get away from here and out of reach of Harry's vengeance, but I found I wasn't able to worry. I wasn't frightened any more. I'd done all that, and it was over now. Poor Harry, though.

I must have fallen asleep in the end. I woke up very late, refreshed by happy dreams, and entirely calm. Also starving. I hurried downstairs.

My mother was there waiting for me, at the best table as ever, faultless as ever. She had finished her coffee and was peering haughtily at a newspaper. She always likes to read what she calls 'the native press' when she's abroad. I'm sure it's an affectation, like giving tips to people who oughtn't to be tipped. I'm sure she doesn't really understand a word.

She looked up when I came in. She was the picture of a loving mother full of concern for her sick daughter. Her expression softened when I filled a plate full of ham and cheese from the buffet and sat down.

'Oh, you *are* better, dear. I'm so glad. Did you have a rotten night? Was it something you picked up in that mountain restaurant of yours?'

(To which the answers were Yes, and, strictly speaking, Yes).

'You should let them make you a picnic here. They're really good at it. I was wondering – would you like to come to Savoleyres with me today?'

This was sweet of her. Savoleyres is the other mountain. Savoleyres is small and low. Its so-called 'red' runs are so easy, you could cruise down them reading a newspaper. Even the native press. With your reading-glasses on. Not really my style. Not Mother's style either, really – she was being kind to me because I was poorly. I could repay her kindness by letting her be kind to me. It's a mother-daughter thing.

And whatever age Harry was going to be today, we'd be unlikely to meet him there, because it's all dowagers and beginners.

'We could go down to La Tzoumaz for lunch, if you've got your appetite back.'

Now she was talking. The restaurant at La Tzoumaz has the best cuisine in the resort. Three-hour lunches overlooking the Rhone valley. I think my reviving appetite might just be able to manage one of those.

'And then, this evening, we've got guests.'

(Guests, Mother?)

'I took the T-bar yesterday, you know what the queues are like, and Laurent spotted me and waved me forward...'

(Laurent is one of the bribed lift attendants.)

'And I found myself next to a charming fellow...'

(Mother, he *put* you next to a charming fellow. Let me guess, he's English, he lives in Chelsea, he banks, he wears tweed and his friends call him Tigger.)

'I went and had a drink with Tigger' (I knew it) 'yesterday evening, and he's coming to dinner tonight, with his son.'

(What???)

'He's a clever boy, he's in his first year at Cambridge. You'll like him, he's reading English and I'm sure you'll have a lot to talk about.'

(Mother, you promised after the last time... Mother, *another* shy ginger boy with glasses whose idea of being romantic is to repeat Wordsworth at one. Mother, I don't care how sexy Tigger is, spare me from his son...)

'He sounds perfect for you and I *think* Tigger hopes he'll find someone sensible to ski with. He brought a girl home to tea yesterday, she seemed nice enough, but when Tigger came out to say hello to her, she ran away.

'He looked, and what do you think? She'd torn up his passport, and run away.'

Mother's attention drifted back to the weather forecast in the paper.

'Now, wasn't that a strange thing to do?'

They

'Look,' Bernard said patiently, 'if you're accelerating, that means you're going downhill. When you slow down, that's *up*hill. You don't need to know anything else. Leave the rest to me. I'm here. Trust me.'

And this time I did. It must have been the fourth or fifth lesson we'd had, and therefore the fourth or fifth time he'd said those words, but this time, for the first time, it really worked. I obeyed him and I trusted him, and it worked. I could ski.

That alone would have been enough to make the day unforgettable. But it wasn't all. That day was the day *they* came.

You don't have regular daily morning lessons with your instructor without getting into habits. That day, as always, I came down by myself in the cable-car after the lesson with Bernard. I went to the café as always, and sparkled in conversation with whoever came in, just as I always do. Afterwards, as always happens, someone escorted me to my own front door. They are kind people.

I sat on the chair next to the small window that looks into the garden. Normally I'd have distracted myself with a book or some music, but now I thought of Bernard's lesson, and I sat quietly and trusted. I sat still and listened. I heard further and further until it seemed that I could hear the whole village, all the way to the distant hum of the lifts.

Closer than that hazy sound was the definite sound of the drips as the hot spring sun burned away at last night's icicles. Out beyond the icicles a bird was singing. Well, you couldn't call it singing exactly, more a metallic 'ting,' like a very small hammer hitting a very big anvil. 'Ting,' then it thought for a while, then 'ting' again. I could have felt fond of it and felt sorry for it too, having so little to say, but instead I envied and hated it, because it could see and I can't.

Except sometimes, in my dreams.

Inside the house, the only sounds were small and inanimate. Boards creaked against each other as the wood moved and breathed. I could hear the indrawn breath of the fridge starting to work and the squeak and rattle and sigh each time it stopped.

By the time I noticed it, the new sound must already have been going on for some time. It was a small sound, quiet and purposeful; and it was alive. There was thought in its movements and in the silences between its movements. It came from the next room. It must be a rat or something, I thought; except that now and then (unless I was imagining it) I could hear a murmur as if a child was talking quietly to itself.

The entire population of Chalet Alyssum was me, my older sister, her husband and their 16-year-old son Robin, and they were all out skiing anyway, so those childish noises had to be an illusion. I was curious to know what sort of illusion it was. When people who see wake up and there's a hideous creature drawing itself up to pounce on them, they can move their head and see that it's made of last night's clothes hanging on the chair, and the light coming in at a strange angle. When you're blind, sounds work just the same as that. If you shift perspective enough, the brain stops pretending that everything you're hearing belongs together, and the monster vanishes into non-existence.

I had to move around and see what happened to the sounds. I hate sitting anyway, except that often the alternative is bumping into things. I got up slowly, and I walked carefully and quietly to the door to the next room.

When I stood by the door, the sounds were louder but the illusion was as strong as ever. Now I was used to thinking of it as voices, I felt almost sure that there were two of them.

All doors have a way of opening them quietly. You just have to know what it is. I'd learnt about this one. I pulled it towards me, pressed the handle down, then pushed the door. It swung open silently – into complete silence.

At the instant of the door's opening, all the sounds had stopped. There was no scufflement or flufflement or loud squeak. Those clear small noises had turned in an instant into clear clean silence.

I went into the room and shut the door behind me. The sound of the closing door echoed off the room's different textures. The corner with the sofa swallowed it, the wall with the fireplace hurled it around a couple of times. I stood there, listening and waiting for the rat to come back. I stood there feeling a bit ridiculous.

Something brushed lightly against my calf.

I jumped, and then there was nothing again. I tied myself into my skin and glued myself to the floor and waited.

The touch came again; and then again, with more confidence. I lowered my right hand slowly and felt something hard and warm and silky: a child's head.

Two strong little fists seized my thumb and little finger and pulled my hand downwards. I sank carefully to a crouching position. The child put its arms round my thigh and I quietly disintegrated. I put my hand behind its head and shoulders and we stayed there together for a bit.

When the second touch came, it was so soft that I nearly didn't notice it.

We got to know each other better as the days went by.

I'd ski as usual with Bernard in the morning: all the frustration had gone, and it was a good experience now, every time. I'd come down and have lunch and conversation in the café as usual. If nowadays I left earlier than I used to, people seemed not to take any notice. I might be going to meet my lover, or to have a siesta. It was none of their business.

I'd get home and I'd take my boots and jacket off. In my damp socks, I'd pad off to the low sofa in the sitting-room. I'd sit down and wait for them to come. I never had to wait long.

In a grown-up room there isn't much for small children to play with, but they did their best. They piled up DVDs in towers and pushed them over and piled them up again. They found the chess set and played noisy games with the pieces. Afterwards I'd go on hands and knees to gather them all together, counting till I'd found all 32 pieces.

They didn't speak. That was odd, because they were big enough to try. The older one must have been three years old at least, but in all their quiet murmurings to each other I couldn't detect anything that sounded like words. Whenever I spoke to them it was my tone of voice they understood, not my words. Like dogs.

The little one was old enough to walk and still young enough to be very proud of it. It stomped. Sometimes it played the gift-giving game, and I'd be presented with a crumpled object and have to guess – was it a present I was meant to be grateful for and keep carefully? Or was the act of giving some kind of ritual that I had to complete by giving the gift back to the giver? Or perhaps this soggy crumpled thing was food and I had to pretend to eat it… Fortunately children of that age are quite used to adults being stupid and not understanding them.

On the other hand, sometimes we didn't play games at all. Sometimes we just snuggled.

Once the first shock was over, it never occurred to me that the children might be real. What worried me was what sort of *un*real they might be. Ghosts I could cope with, because I don't believe in them anyway. Ghouls and phantoms – well, if I were going to invade the earth with rank upon rank of the legions of the undead, I wouldn't start with two toddlers in an isolated chalet in a small but fashionable mountain village. They didn't even smell like ghouls, just like ordinary nice clean well-washed well-looked-after children.

I was worried that it might be me. One hears stories of frustrated women of a certain age forming tragic collections of soft toys or having phantom pregnancies. I'm not frustrated. We knew that we shouldn't have children, it went without saying: I mean, what's the point in producing a baby if you can't even pick it up without poking its eyes out? And whatever 'a certain age' is, I'm not that yet. But what if my mind wasn't listening to reason? What if it was synthesizing phantom toddlers to keep my body happy? It was scary.

In the end I took a bucketful of rationality and poured it on the problem. If it walks like a duck and quacks like a duck then either it is a duck or you should treat it like a duck anyway. So that's what I did. I treated my two little ducks like ducks, and pushed my fears to one side. Until the day when it all came to a head.

It happened to be the day they found the Scrabble set. It was the perfect toy. You could take the pieces out of the bag one by one, or you could tip them all out at once in a lovely noisy cascade. You could carefully put all the pieces in the bag again, one by one until they were all in, and then you could begin all over again. By now I was sure the older child must be a girl, because she was so patient and thorough.

We were having such fun that I didn't hear the front door until it slammed shut behind someone coming home early.

Of course the children vanished at once. I couldn't tell how much of a mess they'd made, and I'd look pretty silly crawling all over the floor trying to tidy it all up. So I didn't try. I got back onto the sofa and picked up my book player. Somehow the earphones had become detached, and I had no time to look for them before the door opened.

'O Aunt,' said Robin's voice. He went smoothly on: 'I'm making coffee, would you like some?' I said yes, and he went out again. As he left he dropped something light onto the sofa next to me. The earphones.

Robin always addresses me as Aunt. It's endearing. Not Aunt Diana or plain Diana or even Auntie Di. Just Aunt. He started it when he was little. 'Is, isn't,' he would say. 'Is, isn't. Is, isn't. Are, Aunt.' Over and over again. In the end the name stuck.

He had another attack of it when he was old enough to learn Latin. Everyone else was learning how to decline *mensa*, a table, but he insisted on *amita*, an aunt. 'Aunt – O Aunt – Aunt – of an aunt – to or for an aunt,' then on a series of triumphant hammer blows, '*by*, *with*, *in*, or *from* an aunt.' Over and over again. Again.

Mercifully, he grew out of that phase too, but 'O Aunt' survived, and I'm glad. We both liked it because it sounded old-fashioned and ceremonious and more appropriate to the Georgian period and to the conversation of antique persons of refinement. We found the idea rather funny – I'm barely ten years older than him – but even when we're on the way to being refined antiques ourselves, I hope he goes on saying 'O Aunt,' just as I hope that he lets me go on calling him

Robin, even when (it may have happened already) he makes his friends call him Rob.

Robin came back, and put a mug of coffee loudly and clearly on the table next to me. 'The handle's on the right,' he said, with his usual thoughtfulness. I heard him put his own mug by the fireplace and sit down on the floor. When he spoke I could tell from his voice that he was looking at the floor and not at me.

'O Aunt,' he began, and hesitated. 'I –'

'Do you think I'm mad?' I hadn't planned to interrupt him, and certainly not like that. At least I managed to make the tone light and inconsequential, as if I were asking him whether my lipstick was smudged.

A heartbeat later I added, 'Robin, if you're going to lie, lie quickly or it doesn't work.'

'I'd rather have a mad aunt than a bitter one,' he said all in one breath, and I burst into tears. It took me as much by surprise as it did him. I never cry.

The Robin of five years ago would have run and hugged me and cried too. The Rob of five years' time would manage somehow; but at 16 he had no idea. He sat there, embarrassed, and did nothing.

After all, perhaps that was wisest. I composed myself. It seems stuntish to cry in front of people. There are so many opportunities for doing it when they aren't there.

He didn't try to apologize. 'Aunt, if something's hurting you that much, I want to know what it is. Please, Aunt, tell me all about it.'

So I did.

Children are dispassionately cruel. They pull a wing off a fly, they stick a sharpened pencil into the back of their friend's neck, they incinerate an ant with a magnifying glass in the sun until it goes pop, but they don't do it to cause harm or hurt. They do it out of curiosity, to see what will happen. Robin wasn't quite a child any more, but he was just as dispassionate. He asked me everything – what I had heard, when I had heard it, what I had done next. What I felt about it, whether we'd discussed the question of children and what the conclusion had been, what I felt about *that*. Sometimes dispassionate kindness can hurt as much as dispassionate cruelty, but it was a good pain really. And sometimes my answers weren't quite what I'd thought they were going to be.

'So do *you* think you're mad?' Robin asked at the end, neutrally.

A straight question deserved a straight answer. 'I don't think so, Robin. It's hard for me to tell, because I don't want to be mad, so I'm not an impartial witness. But they're *not* real and I don't believe in ghosts, so what is there left except hallucinations?'

'O my Aunt, if you were going round the bend, you'd go all the way round. You'd go round six bends. I know you, you don't do things by halves. You'd be having birthday parties for your ghost children. You'd be making us set places for them at dinner.'

I could hear him crawling round the floor putting the Scrabble pieces into their bag. Suddenly he stopped. 'Aunt, can I trust you? Have you really told me absolutely everything that happened?'

I said 'Yes, of course I have,' and he abandoned his task. He came and sat down next to me; or rather, he came and stood above the sofa and let himself go, crashing into it so hard that I thought he'd go through it and through the floor. It's nice to be young.

'Robin?'

'Wait.' He took my hand firmly in his.

Silence.

A soft touch on my leg. I stiffened. Robin's hand tightened round mine.

'Clara,' he said softly. And then again, louder, 'Clara.'

The touch left my leg. Robin leaned forward. His weight shifted. He straightened up again and dumped something on my lap. It wriggled. It was a child.

'She doesn't like to be looked at,' he said in a parenthetical undertone, 'but if – I do – quick glances, she doesn't notice. – Pink dress – brown curly hair – she's smiling.'

'How did you know her name?' I whispered.

'The Scrabble. You learn to write your name long before you can spell anything else. I wrote mine on every wall. Grrrrowrrrr!!' The growl startled me. It startled someone else too, and on the floor something moved. Robin leaned forward and growled again. An answering squeaky growl came from the floor. Robin slid off the sofa with a thump. 'Yes, it's a boy – you're right. – Fair hair. – Scared of me – but enjoys it.'

And so Robin and the nameless boy played a noisy game of bears on the floor while Clara and I stayed on the sofa and tangled our fingers together in different combinations. It struck me how confident Robin was when he wasn't over-shadowed by his parents or his older cousins. It struck me that he'd make a very good father one day.

'It's getting late, Mum and Dad will be be back soon.' He'd even been watching the time. I hoisted Clara gently off my lap and onto the floor. Robin stood up and so did I. 'Time to go, children,' I said. 'See you tomorrow.' And they were gone.

Robin went back to collecting the Scrabble pieces. I thought of something.

'Robin,' I said, 'when you came in and I interrupted what you were saying, what was it? It wasn't about me.'

'No,' he said, swallowing the word.

'Robin, trust me.'

'Yes.' No *O Aunt*, just *Yes*. So, carefully, as dispassionately as he'd disassembled me, with all the delicacy he'll have himself one day when he's older, I pieced his story together.

He'd been skiing with Ed and Zackie, his cousins, most of the week. Ed and Zackie were older than him. They shaved every day and they told better lies about women than he did. He'd been trailing after his big cousins ever since he was four. He'd tried to do everything they could do, whether he could or not. He'd broken an arm once, trying to climb their own special tree. They'd tolerated him and patronised him, and they'd even bullied him a little, which he hadn't minded because it meant they were taking notice of him. My sister couldn't see the harm in it. They kept him out of her hair. I thought they were dangerous.

It turned out Ed and Zackie were going heli-skiing tomorrow. Without Robin. There'd been a row about it over lunch. They had been condescending, and Robin had been upset. I didn't ask him the details. At his age you get more upset than you think you will and you do it quicker than you expect. You're conscious how immature and uncool you're being, and that only makes it worse. In the end you storm off and come home early, only to run straight into a mad aunt.

Whom, as it turned out, he'd handled very well. So now it was my turn. It was only fair.

'I wouldn't trust them,' I began.

'Why not?'

'Robin, I've seen how they behave. Heli-skiing is serious. The mountains are *dangerous,* Robin. Even experts can get injured or lost. And I know those boys. They're immature and irresponsible. If anything went wrong they'd wouldn't know what to do: they'd get over-excited or panicky or try to laugh it off, and we'd have a tragedy on our hands.

'I know you, Robin. If one of *them* got into trouble and you had to stop skiing to help him, you would, I know. But I don't know about them. I really don't know.'

Has I said too much? Too little? I listened to the rhythm of his breathing. It was the only clue I had.

I thought of a plan.

'Robin, can I *really* trust you?'

'Aunt, you know you can.' Reluctantly.

167

'Can I really? Robin, I'm going to ask you something, but it means trusting you with my life. If you think you can't do it, *you must say no.*'

'What is it?'

'Bernard can't make it tomorrow. He has to go down the valley for something. None of the other instructors will take the responsibility. They say it's too much of a risk.'

I went on, putting a little brave insecurity into my voice. 'I'm a very good skier now. You don't have to worry about me falling over. I know which way is down. But there's always the chance I'll take the wrong path. Or someone will be coming down fast and won't see that I can't see them to get out of their way.

'It wouldn't be much fun for you. One eye for yourself and one eye for me, at all times. *At all times*, Robin.'

He wasn't sure if it was his turn to speak. After a moment I went on.

'I know it's a lot to ask. Don't think about your pride, Robin. You must be certain. If you have any doubt at all, Robin, please say no. This is life or death. Really.'

Had I been too melodramatic?

He took a deep breath and let out a bit of it experimentally to see what it felt like.

'No, Aunt, I won't say no. You can rely on me. But – look, if it isn't working or I don't think it's safe, I'll say stop, and we'll stop, OK? I'll get you home safely, but we stop.'

The young are so enchanting when they get responsibility, just like pages at a wedding. I kept a straight face. It was hard.

'OK. But Robin, I don't want to be selfish. If it's too much trouble, don't worry about me. I can always stay at home and look after the children.'

'Aunt, O my Aunt, believe me, it will be an honour and a privilege.' Under the formality I could hear him hiding a bubble of excitement.

'It's a bore to be so dependent,' I said, thinking the opposite for once. Dependence is power, sometimes.

I got a message through to Bernard while Robin was in his bath.

In the morning we proceeded sedately down to the village. I was wearing my bright red goggles. He was carrying two pairs of skis and one and a half pairs of poles, and with one hand he was guiding me discreetly, just enough to let me know where I was.

He stopped by a shop. 'Hold on, Aunt. I won't be a moment. Wait for me. Look at some postcards or something.'

I waited. The sun was warm on my shoulder.

He came back.

'I saw a toy snowplough in the window and I thought, they have so few toys. So I thought I'd get it for them.

'The woman asked was I from Chalet Alyssum and I said yes. So she's given me this big bag of finger puppets as well. She said to me, "It's a present from me. Those poor children must get so bored."'

There was a tone of wonder in his voice.

Then we walked on together, down to the lift station.

All Souls' Day

Captured in the palm of his hand, his life flowed past him. He waited for the right moment and tapped on the screen. Time stopped moving. His finger hovered over the instant that divides past from future. Above it were actions performed, appointments kept, and meetings held: each line, one more brick added to the edifice of his career. Below his finger were the bricks that were not yet ready for use: they were arranged in an orderly stack, line after line, each of them awaiting its turn.

He tapped the screen in a special place, laboriously wrote a few words, and tapped one last time. An icon changed colour. When he got back to the office, his note would be copied to his PC, then archived and backed up: permanent. In a day or two the signed contract would arrive. It too would be scanned and filed away: permanent. One more client would be on board. One more portfolio to manage. One more steady trickle of ½% of its value. If you put together enough small streams, they make a river. If you let the streams flow for long enough, they will fill a lake. Each brick is small, taken on its own, but if you have enough of them… The Romans used small bricks; but the Romans built Rome.

Outside the window of the train the landscape of Switzerland scrolled past, as silent as the screen in front of him and as orderly as his life.

It had been another successful business meeting, but there had been more to it as well. Dinner and an overnight stay, a leisurely morning and a late start. The new client was the son of a hotelier, and his father had given him a hotel to keep him out of mischief. A hotel to play with, and capital too. It looked good enough on paper, but it was only reasonable for the banker to meet the client and assess his prospects before taking him on. Documents would tell you his financial affairs, documents could be read on the train; but documents would tell you nothing about the man.

The visit had told him what the papers hadn't, and it was all good. Energy and imagination and a fine sense of hospitality. Over some excellent cognac they had talked late into the night, about anything except money. They had talked about expensive sports like snowboarding and mountain biking, sports that brought you free-spending friends who were sure to come to your hotel in due course. And as well as those things, they had talked about art.

The banker's economics degree hadn't included a module on the history of art. It should have done. Among the presidents and chairmen, nobody talks about money, or finance, or politics, or the world economy. They have special advisers to do all that for them. The top people go to the opera or the ballet, to productions they or their friends have sponsored, and when they come home, to their comfortable, quietly furnished homes, there is an Altdorfer or a Lorenzo Monaco unostentatiously displayed. It may be worth more than the room it is hung in, or more than the whole house. The people who deal in these things will know. No-one else needs to.

It seemed strange at first to find a mountain-biking thirty-year-old son of a hotelier knowing so much about art, but it made sense when you thought about it. Where there is mountain biking, there are mountains. Where there are mountains, there are mountain villages, and mountain village churches; and that – especially in the Pyrenees – means wall paintings, frescoes, painted wooden ceilings, and the simple pure light of the Romanesque. You can't train hard on your bike every single day, and art is a more interesting way of spending your time off than sitting around all day eating pasta.

Back here in Switzerland there were some good examples too. The church of St Martin in Zillis was world-famous: even the banker had heard of it, with its 153 paintings on the ceiling, and the mirrors on the pews that let you look up at the roof without twisting your neck. But there were other, smaller places that few people had heard of. 'You really ought to stop at St Florian on your way back,' his host had said. 'Just three panel paintings, 12th century, but they are gems…'

'Stop at St Florian.' To do so would be anomalous. It was not on his list. It was not a previously timetabled action. It had not been assessed and approved two weeks in advance. In the closely packed mosaic of his life there was no room for sudden frivolous changes of plan.

He looked down at his screen and the orderly pattern it showed: the days his cleaner came, his three-weekly visits to his parents. There were gaps in the calendar for his girlfriend, the same as the ones she had in her calendar for him. He looked at the screen, and let himself notice what he had been trying to ignore: the tear in the seamless fabric of time.

Today was the first of November. It was a public holiday, the feast of All Saints, in half the cantons of Switzerland. In the other half it was a normal working day. Typical Swiss federal mess. In the holiday cantons half the people would be at work anyway, because their colleagues elsewhere were; and in the working cantons a lot of them would be taking the day off because the rest of the country was. In all this disorder it had proved impossible to make any meaningful appointments for today. The screen covered up the embarrassment by saying 'Do paperwork.' It was an awkward cover-up.

Paperwork was important, of course; but paperwork could really be done at any time. Perhaps he should let one anomaly accommodate the other: the dislocated time and the unscheduled detour. Exceptions call for exceptional handling. Besides, there was an important reception coming up next week. It would be good to be seen to be cultured and knowledgeable among others who were.

On the printed timetable St Florian was shown in italics. That meant a request stop: another Swiss mess. Either trains had time to stop or they did not – surely? Swallowing his irritation at the inconsistency, the banker pressed a button to call the conductor.

He knew all about arriving in places. If it was an airport there'd be a driver waiting, holding up a placard saying DR FRANZ BÄR. If he was arriving by train, he'd be more likely to go straight to the taxi rank and give the driver the name of his hotel. This time neither of these things was scheduled to happen. He would just have to arrive and see what turned up. It felt like being a student again. Back then, he just used to arrive in places because there was always bound to be something. In Milan, once, in the middle of an unsuspected trade fair, there had been nothing but a room in a brothel. He and Urs and Pauli and Maximilian had all shared it. Ten years ago, it must have been. It seemed shorter.

In St Florian, there were no brothels. There were no hotels either, and no taxis. Outside the station there was only the darkening twilight and an unhealthy-looking teenager doing wheelies on his mountain bike. Inside, there was a poster saying when and where it was illegal to pick mushrooms, and a machine selling chewing gum and bars of chocolate. The man behind the ticket window was as helpful as he could be – in other words, not very. No, there were no hotels open just now. There were plenty in the winter season, and guesthouses too, and quite a few in the summer, but now, between seasons, it was a different story. The nearest place that *might* accommodate him was the next stop along the line, 10km away. Trains passed every two hours. Would the gentleman like the next train to stop for him?

The gentleman felt disappointed that his spontaneous moment should have been squashed so soon, and then disappointed with himself for letting himself be disappointed so easily. He explained to the man behind the window that he had come here, to St Florian, specially to see the famous paintings in the church. The man reflected, and unbent a little. His wife had a room that she rented out to skiers during the season. They had just finished repainting it, he was sure she'd be happy to help. Only – looking the banker up and down – 'I don't think it's quite what you're used to.'

It wasn't; but then there was nothing terrible about it either. The smell of paint was still strong, and the two single beds were narrow. Next door, the bath was tiny and the shower curtain was the plastic kind that wraps itself round your body and lets all the water spray on the floor. But it was only for one night, after all. This was an adventure.

Downstairs, he was offered cake and milky coffee. No cafés were open at this time of year, Mrs Gruber explained, and he mustn't go hungry.

'I'm afraid you're not going to be able to see our paintings today,' she said. 'The church is closed because they're getting it ready for tonight's Mass. Our Trudi is going to take part, it's very exciting. She's going to be one of the servers.'

'Not servers, Mum, *readers*,' said Trudi in a how-many-times-do-I-have-to-tell-you voice. She sounded as if she used it often. No-one in history had ever been cursed with such thick parents. Trudi had straw-coloured pigtails and she was going through that stage your arms and legs have grown but not much else has. Her whole manner was that of some-one who would prefer to be invisible for the next year or so. Hide inside your headphones and come out when it's all over.

'Would you like to come to Mass with us?' Mrs Gruber asked; and Bär found that he did. It was years since he'd been inside a church for anything other than a wedding, but it would be a good opportunity to view the paintings without being too arty about it. Besides, it was better than sitting alone watching early evening TV quiz shows or looking through an illustrated book entitled 'Outstanding Beauties of the Swiss Federation.' Yes, the church was definitely the better choice.

In the square the church bell was tolling. It was dark and damp and penetratingly cold. Bär stood with his hosts, wrapped in the all-purpose family sheepskin they kept for lending to guests, and waited for the church doors to open so they could all go in.

The church square was more of a swelling in the road than a proper square. There was a Migros supermarket covered in money-saving posters, there were a few iron posts for attaching bicycles to, and that was more or less it. Not much of a destination, but now it was full of people. Little family groups were standing around, shifting their weight from one foot to another and waving greetings to their friends. Small children kept themselves warm by running around at high speed. Some of them were waving sparklers.

A tall rectangle of warm yellow light: the great west door of the church was being opened at last. Bär kept close to the Grubers so as not to be separated from them when the crowd surged forward. The rectangle swelled and became curved at the top as the doors opened wider. The light was so bright now that it was like firelight and you felt you could warm your hands at it.

No-one moved.

The bell stopped. Out of a nearby doorway came a tall skinny boy carrying a cross on a long pole, then a stockier one swinging a thurible. He was showing off his muscles by swinging it in long arcs with one unsupported arm. As the thurible reached the top of each swing it hesitated for an instant and left behind a fat puff of smoke that shone in the light from the church door.

Beneath the regular dots of smoke came a line of boys and girls in robes, walking two by two. People were standing on their toes or leaning sideways to see their children in the procession; fathers were holding toddlers high above their heads so they could catch a glimpse. The procession entered the church. The organ was playing and from inside the church singing could be heard.

At the end of the procession came the priest. His vestments were shining gold and the light reflected from them left his face in stark shadow. It was impossible to see if he was young or old. He was just a formal abstract golden shape that could have come straight out of an illuminated manuscript.

The priest went into the church, and still the crowd made no attempt to move. We are latecomers, Bär thought, and there is no room for us inside. He never went into churches, but now that he was left standing outside one, he felt left out. If I'd known, he thought, I could have come early and found a seat and kept a place for the others. Next year, he thought, I'll come back and I'll do better. Next year I'll go in.

The crowd didn't seem at all worried by being stuck outside in the cold. Bär couldn't hear any grumbles or reproaches. People simply closed ranks a little, shuffling to get nearer to the warm yellow light, like guests getting closer to the bonfire before the fireworks start.

The strange Mass went on. From the outside, all that could be seen was that welcoming light. From time to time it seemed that there were shadows moving around in it. It was hard to be sure.

A couple of times there was definitely singing going on, because a few people in the crowd joined in. The usual suspects: some women (women will sing anywhere, even if people can hear them) and one or two old men who were evidently too deaf to hear the noise they were making. Not a Deutsche Grammophon moment.

The church bell tolled three times, and people bowed. One or two of the older ones knelt in the slush: without anyone noticing, a few wet flakes of snow had started to fall. The bell tolled three times more, and was silent.

The priest's voice called something from inside the church and people began to turn to each other, shaking hands or even embracing. The children in the square ran about, having a race to see how many hands they could shake in the time. The adults were more restrained: Bär's hand was shaken by Mr and Mrs Gruber, and by a shaven-headed youth with a mugger's face; and by a bent old woman whose eyes, as he looked down into them, had nothing senile about them at all.

The children stopped running around. The snow was falling steadily now. More incomprehensible activity inside the church, and then the procession emerged. The cross-bearer was as tall and straight as ever, but the thurifer was surreptitiously using his other arm to prop up his incense-swinging elbow. Behind him the rest of the procession straggled in an end-of-term sort of way. Now it seemed nothing but a line of children in fancy dress. Finally the stylized shape of the priest in gleaming gold. He hadn't changed. He didn't look as if he was in fancy dress at all.

The dark doorway swallowed the gold as it had swallowed up everything else. The warm light from the great west door faded as the candles were put out. All that was left was an ordinary crowd without much purpose to it, in an ordinary street, getting cold and damp under the streetlights.

Back home, even the dim lamp that hung over the table seemed painfully bright in contrast. Trudi had caught up with them somewhere on the way home, and they all settled down to supper: thick soup that had been left simmering while they were away, and dense chewy rye bread, and heavy, nutty

179

mountain cheese. The hot soup helped, but despite the family sheepskin, Bär felt frozen through and weary beyond endurance. If only I could throw myself on the floor, he thought, I'd be asleep in seconds. He forced himself to keep awake and seem polite and appreciative of the experience he'd been through.

Mrs Gruber, on the other hand, was bright and animated. Something about the whole thing had been very exciting for her and she was trying to get Trudi to share her excitement. To all her questions of 'How did it go?' and 'Did your reading go well?' and 'What did the priest say in his sermon?' Trudi replied in monosyllables that it was OK, everything was OK, she didn't remember much of the sermon but it was OK. Evidently she considered that she had done enough performing for one night and they should leave her alone.

So in the end it was Mrs Gruber who told the story. 'For the Mass for All Saints' Day, we only ever enter the church once. Only once, in the year that we're confirmed. Once in life, once only for each of us. The priest tells the same story in his sermon every year. I've never forgotten it. I hope Trudi doesn't.'

It was in the turbulent times after the Reformation (the story went). Civil and religious affairs were in chaos. Strange sects sprang up that everyone thought had died long since. They claimed secret knowledge that had been hidden for centuries. The common people were not expected to have access to this knowledge, or to understand it. It was not for them.

St Florian was isolated then: it was a day's journey from the nearest road. When a Gnostic brotherhood started to take over, there was no-one to stop them. They were like the Cathars of mediaeval France. They said they had the secret of good and evil. They believed that matter was evil and created by an evil anti-God. The body was not the glory of the soul but its prison. The elect had lived through many lives of purification and with their hidden wisdom they were on the point of becoming pure spirit. The common people existed to work and breed, to serve and to obey. The elect ate only specially prepared food that would not harm their souls. They did not marry, and if one of their selected concubines became pregnant she was suffocated, to save a new soul from being born into the prison of a new body.

Late one summer a traveller arrived on foot, ragged and starving. The people welcomed him, as mountain people do. They fed him and looked after him and made him strong. When he recovered he told them that he was a priest. Quietly and humbly, over meals with trusted friends and friends of friends, he taught them – reminded them – that God had created both matter and spirit, that a human being was not a soul imprisoned in an evil body but a unity of body and soul destined for glory together; that for proof, God had become man; and that on the last day the dead would rise again, a perfect unity of spirit and glorified body.

A generation before, they would have known this so well that they wouldn't have bothered to listen. Now, the priest's words were words of liberation, and they listened more and more, again and again.

But no teaching can remain secret for ever. The second circle of power, the men who were not of the elect but hoped to be soon, heard the rumours. They told the elect; and the elect, too spiritual themselves to condescend to performing any material act, decreed that action should be taken. Family after family found it could not harbour the priest any more. After exclusion came attack, and at last he fled for his life and locked himself into the disused church. It was the 31st of October.

The next morning, the first of November, which had once been All Saints' Day, the church bell began to toll. It went on and on. People came out of their houses and gathered outside the church: the older ones from habit, the younger ones from curiosity. Some people, of course, were there out of hostility. They tried the west door but it was locked and bolted. Some suggested fetching an axe, but others said that it would be sacrilege. Someone from the inner circle said that since matter was evil, attacking it could never be evil. Burn it, he said. They were still arguing when the tolling ceased and all that could be heard was their own quarrelling voices. They were embarrassed and fell silent. A child tried the handle of the west door, and this time the doors swung open and they were free to enter.

It was dark inside, and cold. Three candles burned on each side of the altar and between them stood the priest, in white vestments marked with mildew. Behind him, on the altar, was a gold cup and a massive gold monstrance with a piece of white bread displayed at its centre.

The people came forward and filled the church: the men at the front and the women at the back. The priest waited until everyone was in the church and standing silent, from awe or from prudence, waiting to see what would happen.

The priest turned to the altar, raised the monstrance and turned back with it to face the people. Holding it in both hands he made the sign of the cross over them. 'The blessing of God the Son, of Jesus Christ, true God and true Man, be on you all,' – he paused – 'living and dead.'

The men who were to take the final action had placed themselves carefully. Now they looked round to see that their neighbours were in place for a coordinated move; but they did not see the figures they expected. They saw their fathers. They saw their grandfathers. They saw their long-lost brothers who had died in childhood. All were kneeling quietly, their heads bowed to receive the blessing. The dead were everywhere. Their presence was not a threat but a reassurance, like seeing a familiar face looking down on you when you wake up from an illness.

It was getting crowded, though. The men who had come into the church moved back from the front to leave room for the dead. The church continued to fill up, and they moved further and further back. They found themselves among the women. They were not the women they had come in with, but others, some of whom they remembered. Some were old; quite a few were young and pretty and had babies in their arms. And still the church grew more crowded.

In the end the whole living village found itself standing outside the church while the dead took up all the space

183

within. They heard the priest's voice call out 'Come, it is time to go home,' and the crowd parted and left a broad lane in front of the west door, because the dead were coming out. The dead were smiling and laughing and from time to time one of them would spot friends in the crowd and wave joyfully to them. In the middle of the dead walked the priest. His vestments were bright now, with no sign of mould on them.

They turned left out of the square and went on up the hill towards the cemetery. The people watched them go. Later on some of the braver ones followed but there was no-one to be seen.

'Did the priest disappear as well?' Bär asked.

'No. They found him later and they disposed of him. But their power over us was broken, and when more settled times came, a real priest came out from the city to look after us.'

'He wasn't a real priest, then?'

'Who knows? He might have been a priest. Or a tramp pretending to be a priest. He might have been an angel, or Christ himself.

'It doesn't matter. The power of the brotherhood was broken and we could live once more. Once a year we commemorate our liberation. We can go in only once, like Trudi tonight, but we remember always. That is why we talk about it afterwards, for remembrance.'

Mr Gruber spoke. 'Trudi, what did you see in the church tonight?' He had been quiet for a long time and it seemed to Bär that his question had a bite to it. He remembered that

Mr Gruber had come to St Florian as an adult, fallen in love with a girl here and stayed. That meant he had never been in the church on All Saints' Day. He sounded edgy. Did he disbelieve? Was he jealous? Did he disbelieve because he *was* jealous? There was an undercurrent here. A long-running family argument was being brought to the surface in front of a stranger.

'I don't know,' said the girl. 'I was concentrating on doing my reading. I didn't look.' It was a lie, of course; but asked to provide a weapon for one parent against the other, what else can a child do except pretend to be empty-handed?

There was a certain tension. Diplomatically, Bär broke the silence. 'What about tomorrow? Do you have any special customs for All Souls' Day? In some parts of the world they visit the graveyard, they have parties, even...'

'No,' said the mother, 'bless you, that would be a strange thing for us to do. It's an ordinary day and we get on with the business of it.'

'We start the maintenance of the lifts tomorrow,' Mr Gruber added. 'Some of us even try them out once they're working, if there's any snow. It's a grand sight if it's a nice day. You should have a look before you go.'

The conversation was on safe ground now. How many lifts, what kind they were, how long the season was, how much the maintenance cost. The tension was forgotten and Bär thought that it was a long time since he had had such warm, unaffected people round him. No-one was trying to impress anyone. He thought that perhaps he would be able to squeeze in the lift-mending as well as a glance at the famous ancient paintings in the church. It would be a mark of respect to his hosts, and it would make the adventure complete.

Skiers have a joke about the age of ski lifts. The Swiss buy them and use them, then they sell them second-hand to the French, who use them and sell them to the Italians, who use them and sell them to the Bulgarians... What order you tell it in depends on who you're drinking with, and what mood they're in, and whether they're bigger than you; but the Swiss always come first.

The people of St Florian seemed not have cottoned on to the fact that for this joke to work, you have to *sell* your old ski lifts and not keep them running for ever and ever. The T-bar at the bottom of the hill looked as if it had been in place at least since 'the turbulent times after the Reformation.' Now workmen were crawling over it and doing their best to bring it back to the 21st century after its summer break. The motors were running already. Bär recognised the shaved and pierced mugger from last night, climbing among the pylons, his bright yellow scaffolder's belt full of tools for banging things with or wrenching them. On each pylon he would put his ear to the pulleys, tightening one thing, loosening another. On the ground, other people were testing the T-bar more directly, by using it.

Last night's snow had left no more than a dusting on the ground under Bär's feet. If he wanted, he could push it aside with his shoe and see the tired end-of-season grass underneath. But a little higher up there was one of those odd little snow-pockets that the mountains are dotted with, where something about the shape of the hills means that snow falls harder and stays longer. It happens even on the largest scale. When Méribel is all windswept ice dunes, St Anton, at a lower altitude, is buried under deep snow.

Here was a St Anton in miniature. It must be, because the people using the T-bar had no problem going up it and no problem at all coming down again. Bär, being an orderly character, was mildly shocked at the idea of riding a lift without a signed and current safety certificate for the year in question, but he reflected that unless the cable actually snapped and cut someone in two, a T-bar was a fairly safe device.

They were a ramshackle lot, these skiers. They were mostly quite old. He supposed the younger people would be at work today, but now and then one of the kinetic immortals, the twenty-year-olds with no notion of danger, would shoot down with complete disregard of the shape of the landscape, people's safety, or anything else.

One man in a fur jacket evidently shared Bär's distrust of untested lifts. He was walking steadily up the slope carrying his skis. He must be quite fit, because he didn't look as if he was getting tired. A teenage snowboarder (the first Bär had seen) carved a steep semicircle round him, dipping his glove in the snow as he went. Spiky hair, earring: he looked refreshingly modern.

Suddenly Bär's attention was caught by a movement high up the slope on the left. When we know someone really well we can recognise them from movement alone before you're even close enough to see their face. Even when the mind then hesitates for a long time on the cusp between recognition and identification. Even when you haven't seen each other for ten years.

Pauli had been his best friend at school. They had gone to university together but then, as so often happens, they had grown apart. Or rather, Bär had grown further and Pauli hadn't. That was where the distance had come from. Pauli was the one who drank, and smoked dope, and disappeared for days on end. He'd relied on his intelligence and charm to keep his studies going without opening a book. It had worked, for a while.

The end of Pauli's university career shouldn't have been the end of anything. There was no reason for it to. Once a friend, always a friend. He'd kept Pauli's number in his phone and he'd always been meaning to get in touch. To go for a drink and catch up. Yet something had always stopped him. Fear of embarrassment? Fear of having nothing to say, when once upon a time they couldn't stop both talking at once? Fear of discovering their friendship was obsolete? Whatever the fear was, it worked. When in the end he *had* rung, the voice that answered hadn't been Pauli's. He had deleted the number after that.

And now here Pauli was, coming down the hill towards him. Bär forgot all his fears and shyness and jumped up and down waving his arms and yelling on the top of his voice. The skier showed no sign of noticing. Perhaps it wasn't Pauli after all. Bär stopped jumping around. He felt rather a fool. The skier came closer and he saw that it really was Pauli. Pauli was looking fit and happy, but he showed no sign of recognising Bär, and by now Bär felt shy again. He stayed still. Pauli skied across to the T-bar and rode the lift up and out of sight.

Bär waited, and waited; but Pauli never came back.

He saw the paintings in the end. They were good. His mind was too preoccupied to appreciate them properly, but they were good. He would come back and see them again one day when he was in a better frame of mind for art.

They requested the train for him. It stopped. He got on it and went on to Zurich. His life was still there, waiting for him. It was just like on the screen. A regular life with a regular pattern. He got through it steadily. It continued to scroll past him, one line at a time.

Of course I saw you. I'd have seen you even if I hadn't been looking out for you after last night, I'd have seen you, Mr Dignified Banker, jumping up and down and yelling like some crazy fool. It's been a long time and you haven't changed. Well, you have and you haven't. I hope you still have someone to get drunk with. You need that, you know. You don't know you do, but you do.

We've got a lot to say to each other. Everything – and nothing. Especially nothing. We need to spend a lot of time saying nothing. It can't be done in a hurry. It can't be done when I'm here skiing fast before the snow melts, and you're not. It'll have to wait a little longer, till we're together again.

Now you're back on your railway line to Zurich. You're back on your little hamster wheel that you've made for yourself, going round and round. You're back to being

189

orderly and respectable and not offending anyone. Back to making appointments, keeping appointments. To lists and tasks and tasks and lists and files and files and files.

Where is that line taking you, that line you've chosen to follow? You know a little about art, you must know about perspective. You know that when you look along the tracks you see two rails converging to a point on the horizon. But where is your line going? You don't know. What is at that point on the horizon where the rails meet? You don't know.

Were you never curious about where it was all really leading you? I was. I needed to know. All the time I was finding out, you went on like a chicken pecking a line of grain laid along the ground, never looking up to see if it leads to freedom or being cooked in the pot. You still don't know which.

I needed to know where the line was going; and you can't see it in true perspective unless you go off the rails. So that's where I went.

It's rough ground away from the line, I can tell you that. It's broken pathless ground, a lot of it, and often no-one to tell you which way to go. When you do meet someone, they mostly just tell you to go away.

When you are off the rails there are rocks and sliding screes, and ravines that go nowhere and take you miles off your path. Sometimes you see a peak and you climb it and for a moment you can see the landscape all around, but then the clouds come in and again you don't know where you are.

There are cliffs to fall off, too. As I discovered.

I don't resent it. Well, perhaps I did at the beginning, but not any more. I know my journey was worth it. I hope yours will have been. I hope you'll tell me all about it when we get together this time next year – on All Souls' Day, when the dead come out to ski.